WRECKED

LEIA STONE

To all the Hailey's.

TRIGGER WARNING

Trigger warning: Themes of violence and abuse are present in this book.

ONE

Twenty-two years old, newly divorced, about to be a first-year nursing student, and I had forty-nine dollars to my name. My life was a fucking mess. My first night waitressing at Mickey's Motorcycle Bar in downtown Phoenix was the one ray of sunshine in the recent perpetual shit storm of my life.

"Thanks for hooking me up with this job," I told Angela. I was too embarrassed to admit that this job was my first. By age twenty-two most people had at least three or four jobs, but not me. Bryce wouldn't let me work, so this was my first real taste of freedom since our divorce.

"Girl, of course!" She bopped on her heels excitedly. Angela was a mouthy brunette Latina that I'd been best friends with growing up. She was wearing tight jeans and a cleavage top, complete with drawn-on eyebrows and YOLO tattooed on her wrist. "You picked a hell of a night to be your first. All the cocktail waitresses are being auctioned off to have a drink with patrons for charity."

Fear spiked through me. A drink? Like a date? Even a fake date for charity with a sixty-year-old man was enough to send bile up into my throat. I wasn't ready for a date. Not now, maybe not ever.

"Cool."

I really needed this job. I'd have to push down my issues and deal.

Angela showed me how to clock in and handed me a waist apron. "Girl, I missed you. You went to that fancy school and got married and we all thought we'd never see you again."

Angela was good people. We grew up together in the less desirable part of South Phoenix. Even though we hadn't spoken in years other than liking each other's social media pictures, she'd offered to help me the second I reached out. She had a heart of gold, and to be honest, she was the only friend I had, the only one I could call.

"Yeah ... sorry. Life got ... crazy." Mild panic flooded my system just thinking about the last six years with Bryce. Who the fuck gets engaged at sixteen, married at eighteen, and divorced by twenty-two? What had I been thinking?

I hadn't been thinking, that was the problem. He'd lavished me with expensive gifts, trips to Europe, and charmed my pants off. What sixteen-year-old from the ghetto wouldn't marry the rich class president of a fancy private school? He knew what I needed and he gave it to me, climbing right up into my soul and parking there.

Letting his black heart bleed all over me to infect my every waking moment.

"Hailey?"

Fuck.

"Sorry. Nervous about my first night," I lied.

Get your shit together.

Angela smiled. "Girl, don't even worry. The tips at this bar are insane. If you get to work any of the biker club tables, you're walking out with a hundred bucks for sure."

A hundred bucks—double what I currently had. It sounded like heaven. I tied my apron around my waist and slipped a pen and pad of paper in there.

We made our way out of the back room, into blaring rock music and cigarette smoke, and stepped behind the bar. "Mickey!" Angela popped up on her heels and gave the bar's owner a kiss on the cheek. He was a big-ass dude with a beer belly, over six feet tall and in his late forties. I guess you would need to be big and scary-looking to run the most popular biker bar in South Phoenix.

He was shaking a drink in a steel mixer. "Hey, doll." His eyes then roamed over to me. We'd met for all of six minutes when he'd offered me the job on the spot. He seemed like a nice enough dude. Although he did tell me tonight would be my trial run. "Fuck up too many orders, or go too slow, and I'm going to have to cut you," he'd said.

"Hey, Hailey. Excited for your first night?" He popped the top off the steel tumbler with one hand and poured the amber liquid into a glass.

I nodded, giving him my best smile. "Totally."

Upbeat. Peppy. That's what cocktail waitresses were, right? Not fucking divorced twenty-two-year-old hot messes. I could do this.

He grinned. "Good. I'm going to stick you with Angela all night to train. You'll just be her shadow. Get her whatever she needs."

I nodded and he pointed to a banner that had been taped up against the raw brick wall. *Auction to Benefit Local Homeless Shelter.* "You okay with having a drink with an old geezer for charity?" he asked in a light tone.

I gulped, hugging my arms, but smiled. "Of course."

If Bryce and I were still together and he knew I was having a drink with another man, even to benefit charity...

I had to stop thinking about him, about my old life. I'd broken free of that toxic fucking relationship and I needed to move on.

"Alright, let's work the room. We have some time before the auction starts," Angela told me.

I nodded, creasing my shirt before wiping my palms on my jeans. Why was I so nervous? I was a grown-ass woman, I should be able to handle bringing beers to some crusty old bikers. But these weren't all crusty old bikers. Some of them were hot and dangerous-looking. I scanned the room. Mickey's was a small but beloved local bar. It was skinny but long. There was a stage at the front, to the left when you first walked in. When there wasn't a local band playing, a rock station blared out of the speakers. We had twelve four-top tables and two eight-tops for bigger parties.

"Okay, so we have three waitresses on staff for busy nights. They get left, right, or middle zones.

Tonight, we get left. That's those six four-tops on the left wall." She pointed to our station.

I nodded. Left, right, middle. Easy.

As we walked to the first table on the left side, she leaned in close to me. "Beers and doubles we can pour ourselves, but if it's something fancy, you pass off the order to Mickey."

Doubles, that was a double shot.

Check.

"Cool," I muttered. If I could keep this job and make decent tips, I might be able to move out of the youth hostel I was staying at on Jefferson Street. It smelled like piss and I was pretty sure more than half my roommates were on something.

It's only temporary, I told myself.

"Hey, Johnny!" Angela opened her arms and took some big fifty-year-old man into her arms for a hug. He wore the typical black leather chaps and black vest with his biker gang emblem on the back. I couldn't fully see from here, but it looked like Hells Angels Phoenix Chapter.

"Hey, beautiful. Did you get that carburetor fixed?" he asked her as she grabbed each one of their empty beer bottles and handed them to me.

Angela nodded. "I did. Thanks for hooking me up. Another round?"

Johnny bobbed his head and Angela leaned into me. "Four Bud Lights, lid off," she whispered.

I spun around, making sure to weave in and out of the crowd quickly. Angela warned me that Mickey didn't like lazy waitresses who walked slow or dilly-dallied. If he was watching me, I wanted him to know I could haul ass.

Arriving at the huge beer tub we had on either side of the bar, I chucked the empty bottles into the recycling and grabbed four Bud Lights. Using the bottle popper that I'd hooked to my belt, I popped the caps off in record time. I was going to be a badass cocktail waitress. The next two years of nursing school were going to fly by, and before I knew it I was going to be on my way to financial freedom and emotional security.

Hailey 2.0 was on her way to living the good life.

Spinning around, I surged forward and slammed right into some big dude's chest.

"No!" I shouted as the beers in my arms clicked together and smooshed against my breasts. His chest, my chest, they were the only things keeping the bottles from crashing to the floor and breaking, signaling the end of my first ever job. The dude went to step backward and I pushed harder into him. "Don't move!" I squeaked, trying to work my hands between us, sliding up his rock hard abs to grasp the bottom of the four bottles.

I hadn't even looked up yet, I was so concerned with not spilling these beers and getting fired. When I got a good grip on the bottles, I finally stepped backward and met the dude's gaze.

Holy fuck.

Ethan King. Those piercing blue eyes were hooded as he stared right into my soul. I'd forgotten about Ethan King until this very moment. He was three years older than me and like seventeen years old when I'd last seen him. Honestly, all I remembered were his arresting blue eyes and the intense exchange we'd had on the bridge behind school on the worst day of my life.

The day my mom died. I was fourteen.

"I'm ... sorry. It's my first night," I mumbled. My mouth suddenly dried; there was no way he remembered me. We hadn't hung in the same circles; he was way cooler than me. I was the science nerd freshmen and he was the bad boy senior.

My gaze raked over his arms, covered in tattoos, corded muscles pulling at his shirt almost like it was a second skin. He had a skull tattoo on his neck. Neck and face tattoos were reserved for a certain kind of guy. Like a felon. Everything about him screamed danger. Everything but those eyes. Those eyes were the same ones the seventeen-year-old boy wore when he comforted me outside of class that day I found out my mom overdosed.

Ethan didn't say a word; he didn't look pissed, more like he was in shock, so I was taking that as a good sign he wasn't going to complain to Mickey.

"Really sorry," I mumbled again and took off to bring the beers to Angela's table.

I'd forgotten all about Ethan King, but seeing him now stirred something within me. Something I'd thought was long dead.

THE NEXT HOUR went pretty smoothly. Angela gave me easy tasks, like beer fetching, and taught me what some of the harder drinks were. Like a White Russian. Most of these dudes drank beer or double scotch on the rocks, so it was pretty easy. The screaming over the music was something I would have to get used to. By the end of the night my voice was going to be hoarse. My feet also hurt like hell. These cheap Wal-Mart tennis shoes weren't doing shit for my arch support. Bryce didn't let me take any of my nice clothes when I left. Just what I had on my back. So I was having an adjustment period.

Whatever. I didn't care. I'd wear Wal-Mart white granny undies for the rest of my life to be free of that monster.

"Alright! It's the moment you've all been waiting for!" Mickey called out up on stage, and the crowd went wild. "Tonight we have six beautiful ladies who have agreed to have a drink with one of you sorry schmucks for charity."

Everyone chuckled.

Angela pulled on my arm and we made our way to the small stage at the front. Two of the other cocktail waitresses were moving that way too. I'd met one of them, Taylor, but the other I didn't recognize. They were both young, busty, and beautiful. Seemed Mickey had a type. Hey, if the tips were good I wasn't going to complain. I'd use these knockers for something good, because someday they'd be at my knees.

A hefty woman, wearing a Harley Davidson t-shirt cut down the middle to show her ample cleavage, walked right up to Mickey and the crowd cheered.

"First up we have Donna!" he cried out. "Our

amazing and talented chef. Best onion rings in Arizona!"

Donna bent forward and blew the crowd a kiss, which brought a smile to my face.

"Let me remind you that one hundred-percent of your donations tonight go to helping homeless folks off the street," Mickey growled into the mic. "So don't be stingy, you little fuckers!"

I grinned. The old man was growing on me.

"Twenty dollars!" a young man shouted from the crowd and Donna blew him a kiss.

"Thirty dollars!" another man yelled, waving some cash in the air.

Angela grabbed a giant bucket with a lid to collect the money, and we inched closer to the stage.

"Forty-two dollars and fifty cents!" an old round-bellied man cried out.

Angela smiled. "That's her husband," she whispered to me.

"Alright, highest bid is forty-two fifty. Do I have any more?"

Silence.

"Sold! Donna, go sit with your husband and enjoy a beer on the house!"

Angela moved to collect the money in her bucket

and Mickey reached out and grabbed my arm. "Come on, doll." He gently pulled me on stage.

Oh God.

Second? I didn't want to go second. Not last either. Just a good middle spot where no one would notice me.

"Uhh." I tried to think of an excuse to hold off the inevitable. I had a mild anxiety disorder in crowds, which was interesting now that I'd decided to start working at a crowded bar. My heart hammered in my chest as the men roared in excitement. Sweat broke out on my palms and upper lip, and dizziness washed over me.

Get your shit together, Hailey. It's for charity. It's just a group of old biker thugs.

But it wasn't just the old biker thugs who rode Harleys. There were the young good-looking guys too. One in particular that was burning his blue-eyed gaze into me.

I swallowed hard.

"This pretty little thing just started at Mickey's tonight. Let's give her a warm welcome!" Mickey called out.

The amount of males yelling obscene things was enough to make my cheeks go pink.

Mickey scowled. "Be respectful or you'll be

thrown out," he reminded the wild group. "Hailey is a nursing student—" The men hooted and hollered and had to be quieted down again. "Who has kindly agreed to have one drink for the benefit of our dear charity. Can I start the bidding with—?"

"A hundred bucks!" a tall lanky dude in the back cried out. It looked like his hair was slicked back with olive oil.

"Okay!" Mickey grinned. "I've got a hundred in the back."

"One fifty!" an older Native American gentleman cried out, holding up money and waving it in the air.

My traitorous gaze somehow found its way to Ethan. He was leaned all the way back in his chair, legs spread like he didn't have a care in the world. But those eyes, those eyes looked ... mischievous.

"Two hundred! I'll go higher if she'll wear her nurse uniform!" a man cried out, and everyone cheered.

My gaze fell to the ground as panic rose up in me.

Just survive this night. One day at a time.

"No uniform!" Mickey snapped. "I've got two hundred, going once, going twice—"

"One thousand," a steel voice cut through the space. Silence descended on the bar.

I didn't recognize that voice, but...

"One thousand dollars! Done! Hailey please go enjoy a beer with Ethan King," Mickey announced, and my gaze snapped up and locked with the winner.

Ethan King.

In that moment I wanted to run away from here, from him. I wasn't looking for a new guy—I'd barely survived my last. I knew it was just one drink, but the look in those blue eyes said that it could be so much more.

TWO

I walked on wobbly legs towards the four-top where Ethan sat. The entire time he held my gaze, piercing into me with a deep and serious look that scared the shit out of me. I'd smashed my fucking tits against this guy's chest five minutes ago. What the hell did he think of me?

He probably didn't even remember me.

That sunny day in March when I'd been crying on the bridge between the middle school and high school. Some kids snuck out there in the middle of class to smoke or make out, but I was there to lose my shit over my mom. I'd never forget what he'd said to me.

"Family isn't always blood. It's who we decide them to be. So go out and make your own family." At

just fourteen years old, I remembered thinking he was a fucking Yoda or something. A hot-ass Yoda that I totally wanted to make out with at the time. Ethan had been the one bright spot that day. A cool and sexy seventeen-year-old talking to me in the darkest moment of my life? I'd never forgotten it.

Walking across the bar to him now, I felt like I was walking into my past, the good part of my past, the part I missed, before my mom died and I was led astray. His friends saw me coming and scrambled to give us the table alone. Angela collected the stack of hundred dollar bills from him and winked at me as she passed. My heart felt like it might jump out of my chest. I had no clue what to say. This was a fake-ass charity date, but still ... I was so out of practice I didn't even know how to talk to other men.

"Hailey Willows. I heard you'd moved to Los Angeles," he said casually and gestured for me to sit.

Fuck. He remembered me and his voice was like butter with a little scratchy whisky thrown on top.

I sat, grabbing the beer Angela had handed me before scurrying off. I hated beer. I was a wine and cheese kind of girl, or if the day was hard enough, Jack, but I took a swig anyway.

Maybe Hailey 2.0 could be a beer chick.

"Yeah. I'm back now," was all I offered.

He remembered me. I couldn't get over that. Did he remember our talk that day on the bridge?

Ethan nodded and I couldn't help but let my eyes roam over his tattoos, the tiny scar below his lower lip. Spending the last few years living in a loft in downtown L.A., with a bellhop and men constantly wearing three-piece suits, left me ill-equipped to deal with Ethan King. His jeans were worn, there was grease under his fingernails, and his dark hair was messy in a sexy, I-don't-care-what-I-look-like kind of way.

"Where are you staying?" It was a casual question but one that brought a lot of pain for me. I'd obviously signed a prenup before marrying Bryce, the son of a billionaire, and because he never let me work or go to college, I had nothing in the way of savings. My family were all dead, and the "friends" I'd had in L.A. disowned me at Bryce's command.

AKA homeless.

"In the youth hostel on Jefferson," I squeaked, trying to sit up tall.

Hailey 2.0 wasn't ashamed of her circumstances.

His brows drew down for a moment, but then he brushed it off and took a swig of beer.

I tried to make normal conversation and not

think about how crazy and intense this fake date was: "So what have you been up to since high school?"

Ethan's posture was relaxed, but those eyes watched me like a hawk. It was sexual in a way I couldn't explain.

"Did you hear about my big brother going to jail?" he asked.

I nodded. He had an older brother who'd ended up in jail for dealing drugs. God, this place was such a depressing shithole sometimes. Half the people I grew up with were either hooked on drugs, in prison, or dead.

The last seven years of my life were filled with trips to Paris, yacht parties, and Hollywood red carpet events. You wouldn't hear about any of them going to jail or ending up on meth.

"Well, after that, I started the Kings Motorcycle Club to keep all my friends from joining gangs." He picked up a black leather vest he'd hung over the back of his chair and showed me the emblem. A skull wearing a crown.

"So ... you started a motorcycle club and named it after yourself." I smirked, toying with him a little.

Why was I so awkward? What a stupid thing to ask; it would probably piss him off. What he'd said about starting a club to keep his friends out of gangs made me rethink my internal judgment of him.

A grin tugged at the corner of his mouth, revealing a set of straight white teeth. Men with nice smiles were my kryptonite, and Ethan had an amazing smile.

"I was seventeen when I started the Kings. My ego wasn't exactly in check back then."

Now it was my turn to smile. "But it is now?"

I was talking to a guy and it was easy. Maybe I wasn't such a social freak like Bryce had led me to believe.

Hailey 2.0 was social.

His smile widened and I felt my stomach do flip flops.

"Mostly." He winked.

Were we flirting? I didn't know how I felt about that. The ink had been dry on my divorce papers all of six days. I wasn't ready for this shit. I felt the moment I shut down; it was like a heavy blanket had been thrown over me. My limbs felt weak and desolation opened inside my chest.

I navigated to smoother waters: "Sorry about spilling the beer on you earlier." Topics that wouldn't cause him to smile, or me to flirt.

He shrugged. "It happens."

It happens.

If I'd done that to Bryce or one of our guests at a dinner party, he'd never let me hear the end of it. I'd be branded an incompetent fool not even worthy of serving beer.

Stop thinking about the past.

We were silent a moment while I watched Angela be auctioned off. When I glanced back at Ethan, he was staring at me.

"Did you ever find them?" he asked.

I looked at him, confused. "Find who?"

He leaned forward, bringing the scent of his earthy cologne with him. "Your family. Did you ever go off and make a new family?"

Emotion cut right through me in that moment and my throat tightened.

He remembered everything.

After my mom died I'd become a ward of the state, in and out of foster homes until I emancipated myself at sixteen. That fucking monster Bryce had been the only person I'd considered family and now he was gone too.

Ethan seemed to realize that he'd asked a sensitive question, because he straightened his back and cleared his throat. He changed the subject quickly: "Remember Monica Eisen? She was in my grade?"

I just nodded, trying to rein in my emotions so I wouldn't cry in this fucking bar, on my first day on the job, while I was on a thousand-dollar date with *the* Ethan King.

"She got some big modeling contract after high school and moved to New York," he explained.

I smiled the best fake smile I could manage. "Yeah I heard about that. Good for her."

"So nursing school? I always thought you'd become a doctor. You had the brain for it."

I thought I'd become a doctor too, but now I was too broke, too old, and too tired to go after that dream. I'd applied to Phoenix Community College behind Bryce's back as I planned my exit in L.A. When I got in, I'd been so shocked I didn't reply for weeks. Nursing school at a community college might not sound amazing, but to me it was a fresh start.

"Yeah, I start next week."

I was deliberately keeping my answers short and not asking him about himself. I just wanted this to be over so I could go back to waiting tables with Angela.

Ethan watched me with those crystalline blue eyes. "You don't have to sit here anymore. I just didn't want any of those perverts to get a drink with you."

My heart fell at his words. He'd noticed my shut-down. Why was I so fucking damaged?

I shifted nervously in my seat. "No, I'm sorry. I'm … having a hard time acclimating to being back."

He nodded. "Staying in a hostel on Jefferson probably isn't helping. I heard they hand out hallucinogens like they're candy."

A slow grin crept across my face. "I'm pretty sure I almost drank mushroom tea last night from a sweet couple from Amsterdam."

He laughed and was about to speak when Mickey tapped the mic.

"Alright, folks, I need my ladies to get back to work. I hope you've enjoyed your time with them. The homeless shelter thanks you!"

Ethan reached into his pocket and pulled out his wallet. Opening it, he placed a white card in front of me.

"I've got a little apartment above my garage that's for rent. I could be flexible on the first month since you're getting back on your feet. It's two hundred a month, utilities included. Vacant now, so move in tomorrow if you like."

What did he just say? Move in!

But then my practical mind went to the price.

Two hundred? That was cheap as fuck. Right in my price range. What was wrong with the place?

I stood and peered down at the card.

Ethan King

King's Motorcycle Shop

Owner

With his number at the bottom.

There was no way in hell I was living above Ethan King's garage.

"Cool, I'll see. I might have another hook up in Tempe," I lied.

He nodded and tipped his beer my way. "Good to see you, Hailey Willows."

"You too." My name change back to Willows would take at least six weeks.

His voice, the smoothness in the way he spoke, it awoke parts of myself that I hadn't realized were still alive.

I slipped his card into my back pocket and beelined it for Angela, who was now at the back bar grabbing some drinks.

She shot me a wicked grin. "Ethan King just paid a grand to talk to you for five minutes. Tell me everything."

A nervous laugh escaped me. "Nothing big. Just catching up on old times."

She raised one eyebrow. "Old times, hey?"

"These for table seven?" I waved her off and grabbed the drinks, saying a random table number.

She got the point. "Table ten."

I delivered the drinks and then started to wipe the next empty table down. Over the next few hours of my shift, it was a monotony of serving beer, clearing bottles, and wiping tables. My feet felt like I was walking on bruises, and I really missed my Gucci loafers. But at the end of the night when I went into the back room to clock out, Mickey told me I'd done a great job and he was hiring me permanently.

I did it. I survived my first day of my first job.

I was feeling pretty proud of myself as Angela and I exited the bar. It was almost 3AM and the exhaustion of a full night's work settled into my limbs. I wasn't sure how I was going to be up for an 8AM class once school started, but I'd find a way. I was determined to make it on my own.

"Grabbing an Uber?" Angela asked me as she called her own on her phone.

I didn't have a smart phone. Bryce took it before I left. I'd gotten a prepaid flip phone at Wal-

Mart so I'd have a number to put on job applications.

"Gonna walk, it's just two blocks. I'll see you tomorrow." I gave her a tight hug. "Thanks again for hooking me up with the job."

Angela's face suddenly became serious. "You seemed like you really needed the help."

I sighed, she'd been the only number I'd had memorized from my old life here. When I married Bryce so young, my foster family pretty much wrote me off and Angela was the only link to my past that I cared to keep. "I did. Thanks, girl."

Her Uber showed up and I waved goodnight.

Taking off down the road, I made my way over two blocks to where my hostel was. Like L.A., this city was noisy: sirens in the distance, music blaring out of bars, a homeless man screaming at someone, and the distinct sound of a motorcycle engine. I was fifty feet from my place when I looked over my shoulder to follow the purring of the motorcycle that seemed to have been with me the entire way. My eyes locked on Ethan King riding on the far side of the road, going slow and clearly following me. Two of his buddies were behind him.

What the...?

I faced forward, ignoring the fact that I had

somehow acquired my own protection detail or worse, a stalker.

The moment I slipped inside the youth hostel doors, I heard the rip of the motorcycles as they gunned it down the road.

The hostel was forty bucks a night. Angela had tipped me out a hundred bucks tonight for all my hard work. That would get me two and a half more nights at this shithole or half a month at Ethan's garage...

I'd already paid for tonight, so I was going to sleep on it. Sleep next to my snoring, probably high-as-fuck Danish bunkmate, Agnes. I passed the front lobby, where the hostel manager waved to me, and made my way to room number four. Opening the door quietly, I crept in and used my key to open the footlocker at the end of the bunk bed. The moment the lid popped open, it hit me. After roaming this earth for twenty-two years, all of my possessions fit into one trunk. Not in the cool minimalistic way either—in the homeless, nothing-to-show-for-the-past-fucking-seven-years-I invested-in-a-man way.

Tears spilled out onto my cheeks and I had to bite down in order to keep my sobbing silent. I remembered Bryce stripping me of my jewelry as I tried to walk out the door. My wedding ring, my earrings, everything. Every single thing he'd bought me. He took my smart phone, would have taken my MAC laptop, but I'd concealed it in a special compartment in my backpack. He was so enraged he'd shoved his hand in my bag and ripped all of my clean underwear and jeans out. Like he didn't even want me to have a change of clothes. He wanted me to feel like I was nothing without him, that I would have no possessions without him, all while the doorman watched on because I'd paid him to help me leave Bryce. I was afraid he'd never let me go.

It was in that moment that I'd realized I was capable of murder. Not in the three times he'd struck me across the cheek, or the countless times when he demeaned me in front of his friends, or during the constant verbal abuse. No, I'd never wanted to kill him then. But watching him tear off my jewelry, rip out my clean underwear, and leave me with nothing, that had broken something inside of me, and if I'd had a gun or knife on me, I'd have cut off his balls and then shot him dead.

He made me feel less than human. I would never forgive him for that. After everything we'd been through, I left L.A. feeling like an animal.

I pulled out my laptop and fired it up, then I checked my email. I don't know what I expected to find. Maybe an email from a friend in L.A., maybe more information on the nursing school orientation on Monday. I did not expect to see an email from Bryce: **Subject: Come home**.

My hands started to shake. How dare he? I hadn't even read the email and already I was so angry I could snap this laptop screen in half. I'd had to take out a secret credit card with a seven-thousand-dollar limit in order to pay for the attorney to file the divorce paperwork. I'd had to meticulously plan my escape from that monster so that he could never hurt me again. And now ... *Come home.*

With shaking fingers, I clicked delete before even opening it, and for some reason my mother in law popped into my mind. The last conversation I'd had with her:

"You'll never have it this good, Hailey. No man can provide for you like Bryce can. So he's a little hard to deal with? Go on a girl's weekend and come back refreshed. You'll never have to work a day in your life, and for that you should be grateful."

She had no idea the sadistic shit her son was capable of. His dad owned the biggest PR firm in Beverly Hills, and right out of college at the tender age of twenty-one he made Bryce a partner and gave him a quarter-million dollar-a-year salary. I'd never forget that day. It was the day he bought me my Audi.

The following month he took the keys away for a week when I got home fifteen minutes later than I said I would after going to the gym.

I needed therapy, but I couldn't afford it.

How had I gotten the balls to leave him? There must be something strong left inside of me. I'd need all the strength I could discover in order to rebuild my life on my own terms. But it would taste that much sweeter. I knew it would.

THREE

After Agnes screamed out with an orgasm and woke me up at 6AM, I made a very quick decision. I was going to call Ethan and check out that apartment above his garage. But Hailey 2.0 wasn't taking any fucking favors from men. Hailey 2.0 would owe a man nothing. Hailey 2.0 would live in squalor if it meant she paid for it herself. So if this apartment was lavish with granite countertops and he was charging me two hundred dollars a month, I wasn't taking any fucking handouts.

I strapped on my backpack that contained everything I owned and called Ethan from my flip phone.

He answered on the third ring, sounding pretty awake and alert for 8AM. "Ethan King."

I was standing outside my hostel, unsure where

to go until I had work later that day. "Hi, Ethan, it's Hailey Willows." I tried to sound professional. This was my adult "I am not going to sleep with you ever" voice.

"Hailey. Are you okay?" Concern laced his voice and I hated that it made my insides heat up. A slow burn worked its way from my chest to my belly.

"Yeah. I'm fine. I'm taking the day to look at some apartment openings and thought I would put yours on my list of tours." Bonus of being married to an abusive douchebag for years, I was a damn good liar.

"Oh yeah. Come on by anytime. I'm here now working on an old Harley. Address is on the card."

I cleared my throat. "Okay. I'll be there shortly."

He paused a moment. "Do you need a ride?"

"Nope." I hung up.

Hailey 2.0 didn't take free rides. I would walk the soles right off these fucking Wal-Mart shoes before I took a handout.

Fun fact: when you don't have a smart phone, you don't know where the hell you are half the time. Having grown up here and doing about fifty first Friday art walks downtown, I knew this area pretty well, but everything had changed. New buildings had popped up, the freaking light rail was put in...

I couldn't find Ethan's damn shop.

Finally I broke down and asked a young man who I was pretty sure was a drug dealer. He mapped it for me on his phone and sent me in the right direction. By the time I walked up to Ethan's two-story garage on Adams Street, I was a hot, sweaty mess. My dark brown hair was stuck to the back of my neck, so I tossed it up into a top knot and was grateful I'd thought to wear a crop top that gave my stomach some breathing room. When summer hit, walking and taking the bus or light rail to school was going to suck major ass.

Looking up, I stared at the sign for a long minute, *King's Motorcycle Shop,* hung over the brick front. How did a little kid from the ghetto start his own business? It was inspiring, though I'd never tell him that. When I was sure I wasn't huffing and puffing and my face was no longer dripping sweat, I walked into the front office. A little bell chimed overhead but no one was behind the counter. A small sunglasses display, motorcycle helmets, and an array of bagged chips were for sale in the corner.

"Come on in!" I heard someone scream over music from deeper inside the garage. Bypassing the desk, I saw that a small door was ajar, and it led to a large, six-bay garage.

When my eyes landed on a sweaty, shirtless, Ethan King, I fucking regretted every choice I'd made that led me to this moment. No way could I be roommates with this guy.

He. Was. Delicious.

"Did you find the place okay?" He walked over and turned the music down, giving me a full view of his wide muscular back and perky ass in low slung jeans.

Until this very moment I honestly thought Bryce had deadened anything sexual left inside of me. I had no desire to ever look at another man, more or less touch one. Until now.

"Yeah. Fine." I cleared my throat and held on to my backpack straps for dear life, as if they alone could keep me from the inevitable fucking that Ethan and I would one day most surely do.

His eyes roamed over my sweaty neck and chest. "It's getting hot out."

I was so screwed. I couldn't live here. I couldn't work at Mickey's. I needed to leave the state. Panic ripped through me as our future friends-with-benefits relationship played out in my mind. We'd have mind-blowing sex five nights a week, which I would either love or hate depending on how badly Bryce had ruined me, and then I'd either do something psycho to push him away or he'd fuck up and we'd never talk again.

"The apartment is just up here." He pointed to a set of stairs at the back that led to an upper level.

Focus, Hailey. A man loses his shirt and I lose my mind? Hailey 2.0 couldn't be this girl.

"Cool." I followed his fine ass upstairs and noticed that the entire garage was air conditioned.

"Must cost a fortune to cool this place." I looked at the high ceilings with exposed industrial tubing.

He shrugged. "Not really. I invested in solar panels last year, so I rarely need to pay anything to the electric company."

Fancy. That must be why utilities were included. We reached the top of the landing and I noticed there was actually a huge living space up here. To the left was a door with the number 1A over it, and then to the right was a huge living room with flat screen TV, large kitchen, and another door that said 1B.

"So I live in 1B. It's 1A that's for lease."

He lived here? I would be living with *him*? My mouth went dry and my face must have shown my concern.

"Is that okay? I mean, your apartment has a kitchenette with a small fridge and microwave and a private bathroom. You really would only need to leave if you wanted to use the oven in the bigger kitchen or watch TV." He must have thought I was a fucking nutcase with the amount of rambling he was doing right now.

I probably looked terrified.

"Okay," was all I said. I loved to bake; it was part of what kept me sane during the hard days with Bryce. I'd almost gone to culinary school, but decided nursing was a recession-proof profession.

He unlocked the door and swung it wide open, before stepping inside.

And now I could see why it was two hundred dollars. It was tiny. Like New York City closet tiny. With a twin bed and a desk. Under the desk was a small dorm refrigerator with a microwave on top. This was like a motel room, but it was better than the hostel, and right on my budget. I wasn't taking out student loans for my nursing school tuition; that, and the supplies, uniform, and books, would have to be cash. Ethan walked across the space and opened the door to a tiny bathroom with stand-up shower that had mold in the grout and paint peeling off the ceiling. I was feeling less and less like this was a handout and more confident that the price of two hundred was fair.

A private room with my own bathroom and a lock on the door. A/C included. I'd be stupid to say no.

"My shop hours are Monday through Friday, eight to six, so you'll hear me and my mechanics working with loud power tools. On Sunday and Wednesday nights we have Kings Club meetings and the boys can get a bit rowdy, but I'll make sure they don't bother you or come near your apartment."

My apartment. Fucker knew I was going to take it.

I nodded. "I'd like to apply for it, then. My credit's good but I don't have much in the way of a security deposit. I could give you a hundred now for the first two weeks and the next hundred after I work tonight." I held my chin high. The one good thing being with Bryce had done was give me a 758 credit score. He'd put me as a co-signer on all our credit cards and paid them off monthly, so I looked like an upstanding citizen on paper.

Ethan ran his hand through his hair. "Hailey, I'm not gonna check your credit. A hundred now is fine. Pay me the rest when you get it." He handed me a ring with two keys.

Part of me wanted to retort and tell him to treat

me like any other applicant, but I took them and nodded. "Thank you."

I handed him my crisp hundred-dollar bill from last night and he shoved it in his pocket. "One key works the shop front door and the other is for the apartment."

We stood there in awkward silence, me trying not to stare at his fucking eight-pack and him thinking God-knows-what about me.

"Alright, well, I'll let you settle in." He ran his fingers through his hair again, and I wondered if it was a nervous gesture.

"Are there sheets for the bed or...?" I was back down to forty-nine dollars; I couldn't afford a new bed set.

He nodded. "I'll set them by the door in a bit. I need to shower."

My traitorous mind went to him showering and I put my backpack down. "Yeah, whenever, I'm going to answer some emails," I lied.

With a nod, he left and shut the door behind him.

I sat down on the springy twin mattress and sighed. This was a smart decision. A good choice. But I had a feeling I would regret it. Living with a guy, or across the hall from one, was a messy situation. A hot guy, a guy from my past. I started to unpack my bag.

Six tampons.

Nalgene water bottle.

Wallet.

Havaianas flip flops, the ones I'd been wearing when I left.

Five pair white cotton Wal-Mart undies.

1 pair sleep shorts.

Three t-shirts.

1 pair jean shorts.

1 photo album.

My laptop and charging cord.

THAT WAS MY LIFE. No gum, no pen, not even a pair of earrings or make-up. No flat iron. Nothing.

I plugged my laptop into the desk and played some music. Ethan texted me the Wi-Fi password and I officially saved his name into my phone. *Ethan Landlord.*

That's what he was. *My landlord.* That's it.

After I'd cleaned up my desktop and double-checked my class times for my first day of school tomorrow, I lay back on the bare bed and started to fall asleep. I was running on three hours of sleep and my shift at Mickey's wasn't until 4PM. I had time to kill.

I was awoken to a light knock on the door.

My eyes peeled open and I looked at the clock. It had only been about forty-five minutes.

"Coming." I felt like I was walking through quicksand. I was a two-hours-or-nothing kind of napper. Forty-five minutes was torture. Pulling open the door, my eyes fell to a huge red Target bag. A white note lay on top.

No.

Ethan King had gotten me a gift.

I gingerly pulled the card open and read.

Welcome back to Phoenix. Laundry is behind the kitchen.

-Ethan

I looked left and right but didn't see him lingering around, so I dragged the huge red plastic bag inside the room and shut and locked the door. Leaning against the wall, I stared at the bag for a whole five minutes before I decided to open it.

Ethan got me a present and I didn't know how I felt about it. Peeling open the bag, I pulled out the first item. A brand new pillow.

I sighed and placed it on the bed. Next I pulled out a new pack of pastel blue sheets. Finally I reached in and took out the giant plush comforter. It was a soft pink and blue paisley pattern.

It was a thoughtful fucking gift. But did I just let a man buy me a bed set? Hailey 2.0 was an independent woman.

I should return it. Target was a whole level of fancy I couldn't afford right now. This set with the pillow probably cost him eighty bucks … or more. I shouldn't have asked if the bed came with sheets! This wasn't a motel.

Guilt gnawed at my chest until I remembered one of the rare nuggets of wisdom my mother had left me with before one of her boyfriends had gotten her hooked on drugs and those wisdom nuggets dwindled to nothing. *Never let your pride be bigger than your heart. Accept gifts and give them often.*

I'd have to accept this gift, and when I could afford it I would pay Ethan back or gift him something that cost the same amount.

Yes. That felt better. This was a welcome home gift from my old friend and there was nothing wrong with that. Pulling out the sheets, I tiptoed out the hallway and found the laundry room right off the kitchen. It was stocked with soap and dryer sheets, so I started a load washing my sheets and a few of the dirty clothes I had.

I had exactly $567 left on my seven-thousand-dollar credit card until it was maxed out. The lawyers had cost just over six grand, and although they told me if we went to court I could make Bryce pay the fees and I could keep my Audi, I didn't care. I just wanted out. I planned on saving that $567 for tomorrow morning when I bought my uniform and books for my first semester of nursing school. I decided I would start with the two-year associate's degree and then get working. After I started work, I'd go to night school for the bachelor's degree and possibly even a masters, to become a certified nurse of anesthesia. They made bank. A hundred and twenty grand a year as opposed to the sixty grand I would make with my A.A. Either way, it was more than I had now and I needed to start small—short term goals to get me across the finish line.

But I would need more clothes soon. Angela had said Friday, Saturday, and Sunday nights you made the most, then the weekdays were slower. If I could make another hundred bucks tonight, I might be able to get some more clothes at Goodwill. Maybe some make-up.

Things were looking up.

By 1:30 I had made my new bed, which brightened the entire place. Then I walked to the convenience store and bought three dollars' worth of top ramen, a banana, and a bottle of two-in-one shampoo and conditioner. I showered, dressed in clean clothes, and was ready for a shift at Mickey's. When I walked down to the garage, Ethan was still under the same bike I'd found him under in the morning. But wearing a shirt, thank God.

He stood and stretched. "Going to Mickey's?"

I nodded. "Yeah, thanks for the … gift."

I'd make my late mama proud.

He rubbed the scruff on his chin. "Welcome. Need a ride? I was headed that way anyway." He pointed to his bike, which sat on the far wall.

"No thanks. I like walking," I told him, and beelined it for the door. It was about the biggest lie ever. I hated walking in the sticky heat, but I wasn't going to be getting all cozy with Ethan, and he was being too kind for my liking.

"I'm gonna get you on my bike sooner or later!" he called out after me.

I won't even admit the visual that gave me.

FOUR

"You what?" Angela looked at me wide-eyed while she puffed her vape pen on our fifteen-minute break.

I chuckled at her reaction. "I moved into Ethan's garage. It's not a big deal."

Angela raised one eyebrow. "Girl, it's a huge deal. You guys are totally going to hook up. I give it a week."

I picked at my nail polish and had the fleeting thought that three weeks ago in L.A. was probably the last manicure I'd be getting for a while.

"I'm not exactly emotionally available right now," I told my only friend in the world.

Angela shrugged. "I'm not saying to date him, just fuck him. For me."

I gasped and we both burst out laughing, but then my mood turned more somber. "I'm not interested in that either. I'm still trying to move on from my divorce."

Angela took another puff. "Alright, girl, all I'm saying is when you're ready to move on, move on with him. Ethan's the kind of guy who makes you forget your problems."

I chuckled, a genuine laugh. I hadn't laughed in so long the sound actually startled me. "Why don't you sleep with him?"

She gave me a knowing look. "Because he didn't pay a thousand dollars to have a drink with me, now did he?"

Silence descended on our work break.

"Besides, I've got my eye on his boy Cody. You know I don't mess with white boys."

Another laugh. It was getting easier and easier. "Yeah, even in middle school you liked 'em brown."

She nodded and we were quiet another minute. "I can't believe I got married at eighteen." I put my face in my hands. Sometimes the realization of my stupid life choices just hit me out of nowhere.

Angela reached out and brushed my shoulder. "I can't believe I got a two-year-old kid at home and a tattoo of my baby daddy's name on my ass. We all make mistakes."

My grin grew wider. She was a good friend, and a decent human. I could ask for no better.

Mickey popped his head out the back door. "Break's over, dolls. Hailey, you got some preppy dude sitting in your section. Asking for you."

Everything in my body went numb in that moment.

Preppy dude.

Bryce wouldn't have come here ... would he? How would he have found me? I'd been working here all of two freaking days.

Private investigator? Credit card I'd used at Wal-Mart to get cash back to pay for the hostel? Did he know about my secret card?

Fuck. Fuck. Fuck.

"You okay, girl?" Angela stood and was staring down at me with concern.

I didn't want to bring my drama into my new job. Angela was a new friend, sort of, and I didn't want to hurt our budding friendship.

"Just tired," I lied.

Standing, I brushed my hands on my jeans.

It could *not* be Bryce. There could be some other

random preppy dude at a biker bar in South Phoenix who was asking for me...

Denial was a nice place to live.

I followed Angela inside, all the while putting up the walls that kept me safe, that helped me to not absorb the blackness that was his soul. When we rounded the bar, I flicked my eyes to the two tables I'd been assigned tonight. At one was my group of four young crotch-rocket bikers who'd been playfully hitting on me all night. They'd racked up a couple-hundred-dollar bar tab and I was hoping for a good tip. At the other, Bryce Conner, in the fucking flesh.

We were divorced. I'd served his ass and he'd signed under the presence of my lawyer. The papers were filed, and although it would take a few months for a judge to finalize, I was no longer his. He couldn't hurt me anymore. I'd gone with the fast-track divorce so he couldn't manipulate me into staying. I'd signed an iron-clad prenup and stated in my papers I wanted nothing of his. I'd been hoping I could keep my clothes and phone, but screw it. In the end, I gave it all up not to ever have to see that face again.

The moment he saw me, a sadistic grin pulled up at the corners of his mouth. On the outside he looked angelic. Blond hair, green eyes, good skin. He looked like a Danish Gap model. Bryce wore skinny jeans with no socks and loafers. He was one of those guys. When I got close enough to speak, I crossed my arms and pinned him with what I hoped was a strong glare.

"What the fuck do you want?" I growled. I never spoke to him like that. I always wanted to but I was afraid he'd poison me.

His grin fell and anger tightened his jaw. "Is this why you left me? You wanted to come slum it with these guys?" He gestured to the table behind him.

I took a deep cleansing breath. I wouldn't let him get my under skin.

"Why. Are. You. Here?" I breathed, chest heaving. I'll bet if I did kill him, Angela would help me hide the body. She seemed down for that.

He sighed. "I came to see my *hay girl* playing waitress."

Hay girl. His stupid pet name for me that I never liked.

"Order a drink or leave," I demanded.

His eyes darkened and his thin upper lip curled into a snarl. I'd never spoken to him this way and I was genuinely terrified of him. I was pretty sure he was a psychopath. One night, after one of his friends had flirted with me at a dinner party, he'd burned my hand with his cigarette. He immediately apologized, said it was an accident and got me ice, but I knew, in my soul, that he'd done it on purpose. That was the day I started to plan my escape.

"Bud Light. Go fetch," he whispered.

I took another deep, relaxing breath and walked over to the beer tub. Calmly, I grabbed the bottle popper and peeled the cap off. It took every ounce of self-control I had not to ask Mickey if he had any rat poison behind the counter. I was going to "fetch" his beer and then tell him to go back to L.A. and leave me to my new life. He just needed closure, that was all.

When I spun around, I scanned the room for him, but he was no longer at his table. Maybe he went to the bathroom? But as I walked closer to the table my heart dropped when I saw the hundred dollar bill and note.

I'm staying in town a while. See you around.

For some reason the note and the promise of him staying around and stalking my new life didn't bother me as much as the hundred dollar bill did. He wanted to continue to control me. *That bastard.* I wanted to chug the beer, grab the hundred, and leave town again. Move until he could no longer find me. But that wasn't the way to take a stand. I needed to be strong or this would never end. I slipped the beer to the crotch rocket guys and told them it was on the house, and then I gave Angela the hundred.

She looked bewildered. "What? Girl, why?"

I shrugged. "It's dirty money."

She placed it in her pocket. "Well, I like my money any way I can get it. Clean, dirty, whatever."

I had an hour left of my shift. I wasn't going to do anything to mess up this new job. I'd pay for Bryce's beer myself.

After a few more tables, nothing too rowdy, Mickey cut my shift at 1AM. I'd made $187 in tips and was grinning ear to ear.

I could do this. I could support myself, live on my own, start a new life.

The only issue was ... I was too scared to walk home now that Bryce had shown up. What if he was watching me?

I didn't even have a damn smart phone to call an Uber, and Angela was still working. After chewing my lip in the back room for a full minute, I rang *Ethan Landlord*.

"Hey, Hailey," he said casually, but there was an edge to his voice.

"Shit, it's late. I just realized I might have woken

you." So stupid. He had work tomorrow. He ran a business with normal hours.

"Nah, the Kings meeting just ended. I'm still awake. Everything okay?"

Fuck. I hated this. I hated that I had to be vulnerable to him.

"Yeah. Totally ... just, this guy kind of creeped me out tonight, and I wasn't too keen on walking home if you were going to be in the area—"

"I'll be there in five." The line went dead.

Okay ... Ethan King was coming to pick me up. No big deal. Except, we had a saying in the hood: once you got on a guy's bike, you were halfway in his pants.

This wasn't going to end well. Not well at all.

A few minutes later I stepped outside and Ethan was just pulling up. I did a quick scan for Bryce's white Range Rover but didn't see anything. Was I being paranoid?

Better safe than sorry where Bryce was concerned.

"Are you okay?" Ethan was wearing a tight powder blue t-shirt and worn jeans. There was a bulge at his hip that I was pretty sure was a gun and he wasn't wearing a helmet. His tattooed arms held the handlebars as he gave me a broody look.

His bad boy vibes were screaming "make babies with me."

I had to address the first issue: "I'm fine. Is that a gun?"

Because I didn't need to end up in jail with this asshole and ruin my life. He probably sold drugs on the side if his brother's track record was anything to go by.

He nodded, cool. "Yes, bought legally, and I have a concealed carry permit for it if you'd like to see."

Great, now I sounded like a freaking grandma. I shook my head. He reached behind and grabbed a helmet, giving it to me.

"You don't wear one, but I have to?"

His lips curled into a smile. "Your face is cuter, we should protect it over mine."

Holy mother, a shot of heat ran right from my chest to my pelvis. Ethan was a smooth talker; I needed to be careful with him. Shoving the helmet on, I straddled him from behind and wrapped my arms around his waist.

Sweet babies. His abs were so tight it felt like I was grabbing a bag of rocks.

What was I thinking calling him? I should have taken my chances with my psycho ex.

"Do you mind if we stop at the drugstore?" he

asked. "I need to get a prescription."

I barely registered his words; I was trying not to orgasm from grabbing his abs. How many years had it been since I'd enjoyed sex with Bryce? Too many ... way too many.

"Sure," I squeaked, and he kicked the motor and took off, causing me to hold even tighter to him.

Something happened on this bike ride. This small little five-minute ride to Walgreens made me realize something. I'd never been with a man I felt safe with. Until now. Holding on to Ethan's tight muscles, his gun pressing into my leg, I felt ... safe. It was a wild feeling, one I didn't know I needed until now. One I wasn't sure I deserved, which I knew was a fucked-up thought.

I need therapy.

When we stepped inside the store, I split off and told him I was going to grab some make-up. I liked to think I had a natural beauty, but who was I kidding. Everyone looked better with concealer and mascara. I stopped in front of the Wet and Wild brand before I threw caution to the wind and moved over to Elf make-up. Hailey 1.0 laughed a little inside at my level of current patheticness, but the MAC counter was now currently so far out of my reach, I'd never set foot in another Nordy's again.

After grabbing black eyeliner, mascara, concealer, and lipstick that I could also use as blush, I felt fancy as fuck. I was making my way up to pay when I passed a row of red bikinis on sale. $7.99. I shit you not, Walgreens sold bathing suits. Angela had mentioned her apartment had a pool, and when the Arizona summer hit full blast with 115-degree days, you descended on any public or apartment pool you could. I grabbed a medium even though technically I was a medium top and large bottom. I'd rather my booty be hanging out than my girls.

Once I paid for everything, twenty bucks poorer I headed to the pharmacy to find Ethan. He was just paying when I walked up. The cute pharmacy tech stapled his bag shut and handed it to him. "There ya go, Ethan. Now get home and get that in the refrigerator." She winked.

He nodded. "Thanks, Beth. See you soon."

Hmm, when a dude was on a first-name basis with the pharmacy, he definitely had a pill problem. Probably Vicodin.

"I'm diabetic." He held up the large bag to me and my face fell.

Why was I such a judgy bitch? What was wrong with me?

"I didn't know..." I trailed off.

He made his way for the exit and I trailed behind. "Fell into a semi coma sophomore year in high school. Got diagnosed type one."

Holy shit.

"Is your A1C okay?" I immediately went into nurse mode. I may not have started classes yet but I loved all things medical. Name a medical show and I'd watched it. I read books and medical journals for fun. I'd been on the path to going to med school when Bryce shit on that idea. He "let" me do one semester at UCLA before he deemed that it was too destructive on our relationship and hurt his own academic progress, since I wasn't home at the same time as him. I was such a whipped loser housewife, I just did whatever it took to please him. He was still nice back then, wooing me with romantic trips and gifts.

Ethan chuckled. "Yes, Doc. It's an even 6.0."

Okay that was decent. I relaxed a little. "Is that insulin?" I knew that shit was expensive, even with great health care.

"Yep. A hundred and eighty-nine bucks for about three weeks."

Fuck. That wasn't right. "Robbery," I declared as we jumped back on his bike after storing our bags in the saddle bag.

He shrugged. "I'm just grateful I have the means to pay for it. A lot of people don't."

With a kick, he took off on his bike and I started to reassess exactly what I thought of Ethan Landlord King. Was this badass, tattooed, gun-toting hottie actually a good guy?

Why was he single? I might have to do some detective digging, purely out of curiosity. By the time we made it back to his shop and up the stairs, I was exhausted. We stood there in the hallway. My room to the left. His to the right.

My voice was small and sheepish: "Thanks for the ride."

"Any time." His husky voice was strong and full of promise.

It was a long time before I could fall asleep.

———

THE NEXT DAY I had orientation for nursing school and I was so damn excited. I'd woken up at 6AM full of nervous energy. I was going back to school—that thought alone brought a grin to my face. I'd always loved reading and math, and being raised by a single working mom meant I was constantly thrown into afterschool programs. In sixth grade, my mom put me in a biology club afterschool class and I'd fallen in love with human anatomy.

My first foster family lived in Scottsdale. With them, I transferred to the fancy private school where I was given the tools to succeed academically. When that foster family no longer wanted me—they assumed I would watch their younger children all day like a free nanny—my next foster family kept me in the fancy school. Every single class, I was one of the top three students. The faculty and staff poured compliments over me and told me I was a shoe-in for a full ride scholarship and medical school.

Then I'd met Bryce.

He transferred in at the end of sophomore year and my whole world revolved around him. I gave up everything to please him. Now I was taking back something for myself.

As I stepped off the bus, I followed the signs for the nursing school orientation. Moving among the throng of students, I couldn't help the permanent grin on my face. I'd expected to see a bunch of eighteen year-olds but was pleasantly surprised to see some students my age, and even a woman in her forties.

After sitting through an hour-long inspirational speech on all of the lives we could change as nurses, I went to get my supplies from the bookstore. As I piled the books in my cart, along with a stethoscope and other nursing supplies, the anxiety of how much all of this would cost started to creep up on me. Five hundred and sixty-seven dollars was all I had to spend. What kind of fucked-up world did we live in when the textbooks cost more than taking the class? At seventy-two dollars a credit, one three-credit class cost me $267. But the two textbooks alone for that class were $150 each.

I was going to vomit.

"On a budget?" a blond girl next to me asked.

I gave a nervous laugh. "How can you tell?"

She smiled. "You looked at the price and then made the same face I do. I'm Hannah." She reached out a hand and I shook it.

"Hailey."

She whipped out her smart phone and then grabbed the book from my hands. After tapping in a few things she looked up at me, smiling. "Don't pay full price for this shit. That's what they want, for us all to be in debt. This version is for sale for half price online."

She held her phone screen up for me, and sure enough my $158 book was $74.99 slightly used. Relief washed through me. I felt like such a newbie, I hadn't even thought about a resale site for half-price books. I'd been so accustomed to living life with Bryce and his endless streams of money.

"You are an angel," I told her.

She smiled. "Nursing?"

I nodded.

"You can get gently-used scrubs too. Here, I'll write down the address." She scribbled something on a Chipotle receipt and handed it to me.

I don't know why, but her random act of kindness made me want to cry.

"Thank you so much. Seriously," I told her, knowing she would never really know how much she'd helped me out today.

"Of course. We gotta stick together." She winked. "See you around."

And with that, I'd made my first friend at school and was on my way to a successful future.

Cutting out of the store, I decided to go to the school library and use their computer and order all of my books from this half-price website, before heading over to the store that sold the used scrubs. As I was crossing campus, trying to remember where the library was, the hairs on my arms stood and I felt … exposed, vulnerable. Peering over my shoulder, I tried to examine the faces of the passing students but no one was really looking at me. Still, I couldn't shake that feeling. Bryce being back in town, saying he was going to stick around, had totally fucked with my head.

Once I'd ordered all my books, and purchased an extra-large pair of light blue scrubs, the only pair they had left for five dollars, I headed back to Ethan's.

It was almost six o' clock and his shop would be closed. So far, it felt weird using my key to open his shop to walk through it and up to my apartment, but it was something I would need to get used to.

After a five minute walk from the light rail train station near Ethan's house, there were twenty motorcycles outside the shop and loud music blaring inside. Ethan had said he had club meetings Sundays and Wednesdays, but today was Monday. Letting myself in, while trying to juggle my heavy bags, I locked the shop behind me and then made my way into the main shop floor.

The main power tools and equipment had been cleared and a foldable table had been erected. On it was a big sheet cake with one of those printed edible pictures on it. This one was of Jessica Biel in her bikini. The icing read, "Happy Birthday James."

The moment I walked in, the boys quieted and

Ethan looked up at me with that piercing blue gaze. His arms were crossed over his chest, which made his muscles pop, and he tipped his head in my direction.

"Hey, how was orientation?"

I swallowed hard as twenty dudes stared at me. "Good."

Why was conversation so awkward for me?

Ethan uncrossed his arms and walked over to me. "Want some help with those bags?"

My fingers were turning purple.

"Nope. I got it."

His lips twitched like he was suppressing a smile. "Alright. Well, feel free to join us. James is turning twenty-three." He pointed to a quiet dude in the corner who looked like he didn't want to be here.

After noticing the birthday boy's glum expression, he looked back at me and shrugged. "He's not one for parties."

I chuckled. I felt that. Hard. Unless it was Christmas, my favorite holiday, I hated parties. Probably because Bryce made me throw them and complained about every aspect of what I'd done wrong.

"I've got work at Mickey's in an hour, but thanks." Giving him a sheepish smile, I moved to go up the stairs and one of the loops of my heavy bag slipped from my fingers.

Ethan scooped down and pulled it gently from my hand.

"I'll help you up," he told me, and started to walk up the stairs like it was his God-given mission to make my life easier.

As I followed after him, I noticed all of the smiling faces grinning at me like I was going upstairs to fuck him.

"Man, that room has been vacant for years. Where are we going to crash now?" one guy whispered way too loudly.

"I'd rent it to her too, wouldn't you?" another dude said as the red crept up my cheeks.

Great. Just great. Ethan had totally given me a handout, but I was too broke to care right now. As we reached my door, he set the bag down

"Have a good shift. Let me know if you need a ride home," he told me, and I shook my head immediately.

"I'll be fine, thanks."

Rushing into the room, I closed the door and leaned against it.

Ethan King would either save me or be my undoing. I hadn't decided yet.

FIVE

The first week of school and work just about killed me. I had classes 8AM-3PM every day, then five nights a week I worked at Mickey's from either 4PM to 1AM or 7PM to 3AM, closing the bar down. Only to wake up at 6AM and do it all over again. My days off from Mickey's I was either study-ing, catching up on sleep, or both. I'd barely seen Ethan at home. I was sneaking out of the shop to catch the light rail before he was up, or sneaking in after tending the bar all night when he was asleep. Bryce hadn't shown up, and a few days ago I'd found a can of pink mace in front of my door. Another gift from my landlord. To top it off, Ethan kept coming in for a three-dollar beer and tipping me twenty dollars, so I'd gotten a bike off Craigslist three days ago.

Saturday morning, I'd miraculously slept in until 10AM. I wasn't due at the bar until 7PM and my homework load was light. Could even wait until Sunday.

Let's do something today. I'm free! I texted Angela.

Girl, it's hot as fuck out. Pool party at mine? she wrote back.

Yes! It was supposed to be 106 out. Not too hot that you wanted to hide inside all day, but hot enough that you wanted some relief.

Be there at noon? I'll bring chips and salsa, I wrote back.

Bring Ethan and Cody. You owe me bitch, she replied.

What? Invite Ethan and one of his biker buddies to a pool party? That meant I would have to be in a bathing suit in front of him and he would be shirtless in front of me...

Maybe next time? I tried.

Nice try. They better be with you. I got a babysitter and everything. Love ya.

I blew air through my teeth. Dammit, I really did owe her. Like big time. She got me the job at Mickey's and Cody was a cute dude who worked for

Ethan. She deserved to be happy, I couldn't cock block her because I was running from love, right?

I decided to let the universe choose. I was going to go out and make coffee and if Ethan was out there and didn't seem busy, I would casually ask him to the pool party. But if he was still asleep, it was a sign!

Brushing my teeth and putting on jean shorts, I shuffled out to the kitchen.

And there he was making scrambled eggs. *Shirtless*. In low slung basketball shorts with messy hair.

Why did the universe hate me?

"Want some?" He looked up at me with those pouty fucking lips and I'm pretty sure I stopped breathing.

"Yes," I panted, before I realized he was talking about the eggs. "Yes. Eggs. Please. Yeah," I mumbled and walked over to the coffeepot.

I poured him some black coffee and then made mine as we both sat at the small dining table. When he set the eggs before me, my eyes went to the flower on the plate. Sitting on the edge of the plate was a delicate pink baby rose.

The fucking flower … what was it doing there? I glanced at his flowerless plate and felt totally frozen. Was this a date? Flowers on plates meant something.

"It's just a flower," he said, observing me.

I released the breath I had been holding. "I know."

"My roses are coming in out front. Thought you would enjoy one. Girls like flowers, right?" He seemed confused by my reaction.

Most girls did. What was wrong with me? In a panic, I picked it up and tucked it behind my ear, Hawaiian style.

"It's beautiful."

There was no way in hell I could ask him to the pool now. He'd think we were totally dating, or sleeping together later, or something serious. Oh my God, he probably thought I was some normal chick that had moved in with him and we could become friends with benefits. He had no idea the kind of deranged shit I'd been through the past few years.

"You're not used to people doing something nice for you, are you?" He was looking at me like I was an animal in a cage and I wanted to die of mortification.

Fuck! I wanted to shovel some eggs down my throat and drink my scalding coffee and bounce, not get a therapy session with this shirtless Greek god over here.

I tried for a little honesty: "Not really."

We ate in silence then. Eating, sipping coffee, and just being. It was nice to not have to think of anything to say. I didn't feel a weird pressure I usually felt to keep a conversation going with someone new. I just tried to stop thinking about the flower.

"How's school?" he asked after a while.

A grin broke out on my face. "It's time-consuming but ... I love it. Did you know that tooth enamel is the hardest substance in the human body?"

Now it was his turn to smile. "I did not."

I was about to bring up another cool medical factoid when his phone buzzed. He glanced at it and then met my gaze.

"Angela said there is a pool party at noon and you're going?" he queried.

That little bitch.

I laughed nervously. "I was going to invite you. And Cody. But then I thought you might be busy and..." Why was I so awkward? Why did he have to give me this stupid flower?

"And I put a flower on your plate and now you think I want to marry you," he finished, watching me behind dancing, mischievous eyes.

My eyes widened. "What? No. I..."

Deep laughter emanated from his chest and I couldn't help but feel happy myself. Ethan had a contagious energy about him, even when he was saying crazy things that made me uncomfortable.

"I'll check with Cody. We'll see if we can make it." He tipped the rest of his coffee back in one swallow and stood, throwing his plate in the sink before slipping into his bedroom without another word.

What the hell just happened? Why was I reading into shit with him so much? It's not like he knew I was going to come out and had planned some big breakfast. He saw me walk over and snapped off a flower. Would I have had the same reaction if Mickey did the same? No. I would have thought it was sweet and thanked him.

Fuck.

Feeling totally frazzled, I made my way back to my room to shower and slip into my $7.99 suit. As I predicted, the girls were snug in their holders but my ass looked like it was eating the poor red cloth. The bottoms were now a mixture between full butt coverage and a thong. Nothing I could do about it now. After pulling on my only pair of shorts and my Havaiana's, I left Ethan's on my bike and headed to the market on the corner to get chips and salsa. Bryce had engrained being a good hostess into me and I was taught to never show up to a party empty handed.

I locked up my bike and chatted up Miguel, the shop owner, before buying the chips and salsa. When I stepped out to set the bag of food in my bike's front basket, I noticed it was already full. With a gift.

A gift I recognized.

I spun around, pulling the pink mace from my keychain, ready to spray Bryce right in the face if he were behind me, but there was no one. Just the brand new Louis Vuitton purse tucked in its brown cloth sack with certificate of purchase. I couldn't believe I used to fall for these things, used to think this meant he loved me.

Gripping the bag in my shaking fingers, I thought for two seconds about returning it and paying off my credit card. Then I thought about giving it to Angela, but I settled for throwing it on the ground and peddling off in a storm of emotions.

Bryce Connor would not undo all of the progress I had made without him. I wouldn't allow it.

"WAIT A SECOND. You fucking threw a genuine Louis Vuitton purse on the ground just now?" Angela and I were sitting on the top step of the pool, drinking margaritas she'd made and talking. I decided I needed an ally in this fight with Bryce; someone needed to know he was ... stalking me. Because that's what it was at this point.

I nodded.

She stood. "What street, girl? I'm gonna go see if it's still there."

Laughter pealed out of me. "No. He was probably watching. It's gone now I'm sure."

Her eyes darkened. "That's some creepy shit. You should go to the cops."

I laughed. "Yeah, Officer, my ex-husband is trying to woo me back into his life with expensive gifts. Help me."

She frowned, taking a long chug of her frozen drink. "Yeah, okay that doesn't sound so scary. But you should tell Ethan."

My eyes bugged. "No way. Promise me you won't say anything! He already thinks I'm such a nutcase."

She was quiet a minute. "Alright, but you have to promise to tell me if L.A. douchebag does anything else creepy."

I nodded. "Promise."

Angela could be my ally. She could keep my secrets and be a good barometer of how psycho Bryce really was. I'd become slightly immune to it.

"So are they coming or what?" she asked, readjusting her boobs for maximum cleavage effect. Angela was gorgeous, and sweet. Cody would be crazy not to be into her.

I threw up my arms. "Don't know. He said he'd try."

After he put a rose on my breakfast plate and I took it as a sign we were a couple.

"And try he did," Angela grinned, looking at something behind me.

Turning slowly, I took in his form. Wearing a baseball hat, no shirt, and the lowest swim shorts I'd ever seen, Ethan King was walking towards me.

Kill me now.

In his hands were a small cooler and a bunch of roses from his fucking garden. The same roses I'd freaked out about. Walking beside him, Cody wearing a big smile.

"Hola, chicas!" Cody called out and ran towards the edge of the pool before diving in, splashing us both.

Angela burst into a peal of laughter and swam

after Cody. No shame in her game, she was going for it. I on the other hand was resisting the urge to look down and see if my boobs looked okay, or if my stomach was rolled over since I was sitting.

Ethan walked to the edge of the pool and extended the handful of wild roses to Angela. "A gift for the lovely hostess."

She smiled, taking the flowers. "Ethan, you're sweeter than honey," she gushed and then looked over at me to give me a wink.

Yeah. He was. And I'd totally misinterpreted his sweetness for something it wasn't. He was that nice guy who treated every girl like a queen. They were so rare that I didn't even know how to recognize them anymore. I wasn't any more special to him than Angela was. That calmed me and made me yearn for him at the same time. Something inside of me was definitely broken. I was hot and cold. Wanting to jump on him and push him away at the same time.

"I thought we could grill." Ethan held up the cooler, pulling me out of my thoughts.

I stood up from the pool step and wrapped a towel around my waist. "Perfect, I'll help."

He set the cooler on the picnic table and went to tend the barbeque. The pool was pretty dead but for an older woman reading a steamy romance novel, now peeking over her book at Ethan.

I didn't blame her.

I opened the cooler to pull out the burgers and saw Ethan's insulin pen wrapped in a baggie. It must be stressful living with a chronic condition. He couldn't even go to a pool party without bringing his medication on ice...

Looking up, I watched him squat down and light the fire and found myself thinking about that rose on my plate this morning, about the bushel he'd given Angela. It was a simple and sweet gesture, one that didn't cost him money, and it had affected me. Then my mind went to the Louis Vuitton purse in my bike basket and I turned to look over my shoulder. When would Bryce go home? Why the fuck was he even here?

Grabbing the burger meat, I walked over to the grill and handed it to Ethan.

"You know I make a mean burger with bits of onion, carrot, and cheese mixed in," I told him.

He scrunched his face up. "Carrot?"

I laughed and bumped his hip with mine, moving him out of the way. "It's good!" I laid out the burgers evenly on the grill as he watched me.

"I've never let a woman take over my grill before." His voice was husky next to me, and I froze.

"Shit. I'm sorry." I turned to face him and there was a fire in his eyes, a passion that sent a pool of warmth right between my legs.

"I'm used to doing all the cooking." I rubbed my hands together nervously. Did Ethan even know I'd been married before? I'm sure he'd heard the rumors. Bryce wouldn't lift a finger even to save his life. I cooked. I cleaned. I did it all. I was a fucking eighteen-year-old housewife; my wild twenties were taken from me.

Ethan took one step closer to me and I wasn't sure if it was him or the heat of the grill but I thought I might burn up in that moment.

"Why don't you go relax and let me serve you?" he whispered.

Let me serve you.

Something about that sentence unraveled a part of me. Ethan King was a good guy wearing a bad boy mask and I wanted that in the worst way.

"Okay..." I was lost for words. I was a helper, a doer, I didn't sit around while gorgeous half-naked men cooked for me and *served* me.

I was buying a vibrator. Tomorrow. It was the

only thing that would keep me from sneaking into Ethan's room and taking what I wanted.

Deciding I needed to cool off, I threw my towel on the chair and jumped into the pool, fully submerging. What was happening to me? I hadn't felt this way about a man in ... forever. Bryce was my first and only "love" and it had become very apparent to me early on in our marriage that wasn't real love. I'd lost my virginity to him and he was the only man I'd been with since. Sex in the beginning was fun, as fun as sex can be with a sixteen-year-old boy, fast and hard and over too quickly. As our marriage soured, our sex became rough when he was mad, and always obligational. In the end, I started to sleep in the guest room, and stayed there for the past six months. I closed down emotionally to him, and thought that the passionate, sexy part of me was dead ... until now.

When I broke for air, I found myself stealing glances at Ethan. Watching him tend the grill, I wondered what kind of lover he would be. Fast? Hard? I doubted it. If he could promise me that we could sleep together casually and no one would get hurt, I would peel off this red bikini and take him right here. But no one could promise that and I wasn't sure I could survive another trauma to my heart.

He never had girls over.

He'd never raised his voice to me.

He was always there when I asked.

He'd made me breakfast and had given me a rose.

Ethan King was a fucking good guy from what I could see, and that was dangerous for me. I could fall into the arms of a good guy and let him patch me up; I could be safe and trust and love a good guy. And then when the good guy broke up with me, I wouldn't survive it. Not like I survived Bryce. It was easy to get over Bryce. We'd been over for a long time. He was an abusive sadistic monster whom I hadn't loved for years. But a good guy? A good guy would wreck me.

My walls came up then. Up and down, up and down, that's how they worked. I didn't want to be broken again, I couldn't let this attraction to Ethan damage me when I was so fragile.

"Burgers' ready!" Ethan called, and Angela swam over to me while Cody popped out of the pool.

"Hey, Cody just invited me to the movies later. You working?"

I nodded. "But have fun." I tried to smile. Smiling was fake when my walls were fully up.

We walked over to the table and Ethan asked me what I wanted on my burger while he delicately added cheese and light ketchup at my request. Because that's what good guys did. He made Angela's burger too.

"How long have you guys known each other?" Angela asked the boys as she tucked into her burger.

Cody was my age. He placed an arm around Ethan. "I've known this fool since I was fifteen. He invited me to a Kings club meeting in his dad's garage. Kept me from joining a gang."

Ethan gave him a slight smile. "Yet you still managed to get arrested on New Year's Eve."

Cody cracked up. "Why you gotta bring that shit up? The pig was asking for it."

Ethan side-glanced his buddy with a grin, dark hair tousled wildly.

Angela playfully smacked Cody's shoulder. "What did you do?"

Cody gave a noncommittal shrug. "I may or may not have peed on a cop's car."

We all busted up laughing.

"That was stupid," I joked.

Cody nodded. "I was so hammered and he was talking shit about my bike."

Ethan took a bite of burger but continued to watch his friend with mischievous eyes. "You knocked out the bail jar for a solid year with that one, bro."

I put my hand out. "Hold up. You have a bail jar?"

Both boys shared a knowing look. "Part of the monthly club dues go into a legal fund. AKA the bail jar for whichever idiot needs it next."

"Have you needed it?" I chuckled.

Silence descended between the two men and I immediately regretted my question. Cody stared at his burger awkwardly and Ethan looked right at me with the most serious face I'd ever seen. His mouth was slack and he looked despondent.

"Once," he said finally.

Angela and I were silent. My stupid mouth ... who asks questions like that? Oh, hey, so ... any felonies? He was the leader of a biker gang. Of course he'd been to jail.

"But I'm not proud of it," he added.

The question of what he'd gotten arrested for was burning a hole in my tongue, but I bit it down and changed the subject. "I'm doing my first blood draw next week. Pretty nervous."

Angela moved the conversation with me: "Girl, you better not blow someone's vein."

"You'll do great," Ethan declared, causing Angela to give me a funny look while I proceeded to shove the rest of the burger down my throat.

Felon, check.

Nice guy, check.

Fuckable, check.

I was so screwed.

SIX

After we swam and ate a bit more, we all dispersed back home. I needed to shower and get ready for my shift at Mickey's. Ethan had insisted on following me from Angela's to the shop on his bike, even though I'd had a whopping one margarita. Hearing the purr of his bike just behind me while I rode home made me wonder if this was what a normal relationship would be like. If Ethan and I were dating, he would probably be all protective and shit. But not in the domineering psycho way that Bryce was.

Maybe I should switch my major to psychology. Save on therapy bills.

After showering and dressing in a cute royal blue sundress I'd scored at Goodwill, with some slightly used all black Nikes, I ran a curling iron through my hair. Goodwill smelled like shit but you could find some seriously good stuff there. Rich people just gave shit to them like it was no big deal and I was definitely reaping the benefits of that. This dress was Express brand and I paid $4.99. The Nikes looked barely worn and were $11.99. I might never shop at a full price store again. It was just a waste of money.

After stuffing my mace, wallet, and flip phone in my new/used purse I headed to the kitchen to grab a protein shake.

Ethan was sitting at the table, a bunch of papers spread out before him.

"Going back to school?" I joked as I grabbed the protein shake from the fridge.

He looked up at me, his gaze running from my curled hair, down my chest to my ankles and I nearly melted.

"No, I'm not book smart like you. These are my quarterly taxes for the shop. When you own your own business, Uncle Sam wants to be paid every few months."

His book smart comment bothered me, like he didn't think he was smart. "You don't have to be book smart to be successful. Look what you've done with this place." I gestured around the shop. Every time I came out during business hours, it was full and seemed to be thriving.

He nodded. "Inner city small business loan got me started. We were in the red for the first year. Finally turned a profit after that. It's been hard work and late hours, but it's not really working if you do what you love."

There was nothing sexier than a guy who was passionate and driven. He didn't need to be a millionaire.

"You should be very proud."

He nodded. "And so should you. Starting school when most would say it's too late, working full time and take a full class load. It's inspiring."

His words sucked up all the air between us and I suddenly felt so *seen*. Like someone actually saw all of my hard work and determination...

"Alright, well, I've got a shift at Mickey's. You stopping by later?" I changed the subject to something lighter. I couldn't go there with him yet. I wasn't ready to tell him my story. He and the Kings usually came by on Saturday nights, so it was a good bet he would be by tonight.

He nodded over his stack of papers, looking at me over a hooded gaze and those damn long lashes. "Once I get through this, yeah. I'll see you there."

I smiled. "'Kay."

I turned to leave when he said my name. Hearing my name on his lips did something to me, especially when he said it so softly.

Spinning around, I noticed a dark and haunted look on his face. "I wanted to explain about earlier when you asked about me being arrested."

Oh God.

He was going deep with me. He was going to tell me his story.

"You don't have to. I shouldn't have asked." I held my protein shake, willing it to spill or create a diversion somehow so that whatever was about to come out of Ethan's mouth wouldn't. I didn't want to bond with him any more than I already had. I didn't want to feel closer.

"My dad used to beat on my mom." His statement made the room spin and I found myself walking over to him, sitting down at the table and reaching out to touch his hand.

He'd dropped the bomb. He was telling me things he probably hadn't told most people in his life. And I didn't know what to do with it.

"When I was younger there wasn't much I could do. My dad's a big dude and he's always packing."

Fucking Christ. This story was going to gut me. I

knew it. Yet I couldn't turn away, I didn't want him to stop. I wanted to know what Little Ethan went through, what turned him into the sweet man he was today. Was it the love he had for his mother?

He sighed and rubbed the back of his neck. "One night, just before I was about to turn eighteen, I heard them fighting. I stepped out of my room to distract him before the fight could get bigger, when I heard the smack of fist on bone."

My entire body flinched and I ripped my hand from his to cup my cheek. I'd never forget that sound. The sound it made when Bryce first hit me.

Ethan was staring at the kitchen tiles now and didn't realize the effect his story had on me.

His voice was low and deadly, causing goose-bumps to break out on my arms. "I fucking went berserk. I beat him within an inch of his life."

Normally hearing a man say that he beat another man within an inch of his life would scare the shit out of me, but hearing it from Ethan ... it made me feel safer. Probably another talking point for my eventual therapy session.

"I'm so sorry." I reached out and squeezed his fingers. "Did you go to jail?"

Ethan met my eyes now and there was a storm going on there. "Just thirty days in juvie, but they had to put it on my record, felony assault, because I was almost eighteen. Had it later expunged because it was ruled self-defense. My mom dropped charges on my dad if he would drop charges on me."

Jesus. So dysfunctional. But I didn't have room to talk. For a while there I grew up thinking crack pipes were mommy's clear cigarettes, or her "candy" as she would call it. I missed her love when she was available and sober enough to give it, but moving in with my foster family to a nicer part of town was probably the best thing that could have happened to me. Even if it led me to Bryce.

It took me a moment to realize we were still holding hands. Ethan was looking at our interlocked fingers with an unreadable expression. In a panic, I pulled my fingers back and rubbed my hands together.

My voice was small: "Thanks for sharing that with me."

He nodded. "I didn't want you thinking I was a murderer or drug dealer or anything."

I grinned. "Except for that weed bust in eighth grade."

That brought a smile to his lips. "You heard about that? Hey, that was my big brother's fault. He stashed it in my backpack."

"Mmm hmm, sure." I winked.

He was still smiling. "You want a ride? You might be late at this point."

I checked my watch. *Shit!* "You mind?"

Standing up, he grabbed his bike keys. "Never. The more I drive around town with a pretty girl on the back of my bike, the more it raises my clout."

I couldn't help but laugh, he was funny. He was always making me laugh or smile, something I wasn't used to.

As we passed the stairway, one of his hoodies was draped over it. He grabbed it and handed it to me.

I frowned, looking at it, confused.

"To tie around your waist. You're wearing a dress." He actually blushed, which I liked seeing. I didn't want to inform him that if anyone saw my big-ass Wal-Mart granny panties, it wouldn't do much for them, so I just tied it around my waist. The fact that he cared about my modesty was more than slightly adorable and I was very terrified that I was actually falling for him. Not just in a want to fuck your landlord way. I wanted to have something with Ethan, something normal couples had. But I just wasn't sure I was ready or capable and that shit made me sad.

After dropping me off at work, Ethan took off back to the shop to finish his taxes and I kept my mind busy with beer pimping and mild flirting for tips. Angela wasn't working today, but Taylor was pretty cool and the night was flying by. Mickey had given me six tables tonight and we were packed. I could almost taste the money I was going to make. Maybe I'd put it in the budget to buy some Target level undies. With lace. Fancy up my undergarments just in case a certain tattooed felon ever saw them.

A normal person should probably wait a year after divorcing before even thinking about moving on, but Bryce had been dead to me for so long I felt like moving on was all I could think about now.

I was so busy I didn't even notice when Ethan and his boys came in. They were sitting at a table in my section. Sebastian was there; he was the shop manager. And so were Nick, the short wild one of the group, and James, the tall silent one.

"Hey, boys! Can I start you off with a round?" I set some napkins and a bowl of pretzels at their table.

Nick winked at me. "Bud Lights for all of us please, beautiful." He was the flirter in the group and constantly trying to make passes at all the waitresses here.

"You got it."

I moved to pass their table and head back to the beer tubs when a hand snaked out and grabbed my upper arm. Hard.

Looking up, my gaze flicked up to the hardened lines of Bryce's face. By the smell of his breath he was drunk.

"Let go!" I pulled my arm back, but he didn't lessen his grip.

"You didn't like my gift?" he growled.

When the fuck did he get here?

"Ow." I tried to pull back again—the skin of my underarm was getting pinched between his fingers—when a tattooed blur streaked past me and plowed into Bryce, who released his grip and flew backwards.

"She said let go, you fuckin' punk!" Ethan's voice was deadly. Bryce was laid out on the ground, Ethan hovering over him, breathing in and out deeply.

"We got a problem, boys?" Mickey shouted over the music and reached for something under the bar counter and I instinctively knew it was a gun.

Bryce stood, brushing off his pants and squared his shoulders. There was venom in his gaze. "Just having a little chat with my wife."

Motherfucker. How dare he come in and try to ruin this new job for me. My eyes flicked to Ethan, whose face was slack with shock, but only for a moment before it was once again replaced with a cool and deadly calm.

"Ex-wife," I growled.

Mickey rolled his eyes. "Take it outside!" He'd deemed our little spat as a non-issue, something for which I was grateful.

Ethan took a step closer to Bryce. "You wanna do that? You wanna step outside with me?"

Oh fuck.

I beat him within an inch of his life, played out in my head over and over.

Bryce had an ego the size of an elephant. Even if it would kill him, he would never back down to Ethan. Did I want Bryce out of my life? Yes. But did I want my hottie felon landlord to wind up in prison for life over me? No.

I stepped in front of Ethan. "I've got this." My voice didn't shake, something for which I was very proud.

"He hurt you." The veins in Ethan's neck were bulging, fists clenched. I felt like I was witnessing Bruce Banner trying to talk down the Hulk from coming out.

"I know, and if he does it again, I'll cut his fucking throat out," I growled. I didn't mention that I didn't have a knife, nor did I think I was capable of cutting someone's throat out, but it sounded badass and it made me feel better.

Bryce grinned. "I love when she gets feisty like that. Don't you?" he asked Ethan.

Ethan stepped forward again and I pressed my back into him to keep him from getting too close to Bryce.

I pointed to the door. "Bryce, get the fuck outside before I have you thrown out."

"Only if you walk me out." Bryce was the master manipulator. When we argued and I tried to leave the bedroom to sleep in the guest room, he would somehow con me back into falling asleep at his side.

"Oh, I'll walk you out. For the last time, Bryce, I'm walking you out of my life." I pointed to the door again and Ethan fell back to let him pass.

I wasn't going to be the scared timid girl anymore. I wasn't going to be his punching bag. These few weeks on my own had shown me just how strong I was.

Bryce walked to the front door where Colin, our bouncer, opened it for us. "I'm right here if you need me," Colin said.

He must have watched the whole thing.

Peering over my shoulder, I saw those piercing

blue eyes. I knew Ethan was there if I needed him too, and that helped.

When we got outside and the music was dulled, I noticed the black hired sedan that had to be Bryce's. When he drank a lot, he couldn't do an Uber or taxi, no; he hired a fucking servant driver like the rich douchebag he was.

"Bryce, it's over. We're done. Go back to L.A. and leave me alone." I stood firm and said all of the things I wanted to say when I walked out a few weeks ago but had been too scared. He'd only signed the divorce papers because my team of six-thousand-dollar lawyers were hovering over him. His pride wouldn't allow him to beg me to stay before such distinguished men.

"Come home." He completely didn't listen to a word I fucking said.

I sighed. "I am home. Go find someone else's life to ruin. I'm fucking done with you."

I turned to walk inside when his ominous voice reached out to me. "But I'm not done with you." I froze, chills working up my arms.

When I spun around, his car took off. He was gone, and I hated to admit it, but he'd scared me shitless.

I'm not done with you.

When I walked back inside, my hands were shaking a little, but I put a smile on my face. I walked right past Ethan's table and up to the bar. "Sorry, Mickey. Won't happen again."

I needed this fucking job.

"It's okay, doll. Isn't the first and won't be the last. You okay?"

I nodded.

Reaching over to the beer tub, I grabbed four Bud Lights and popped the tops.

I'm not done with you played over and over in my head as I walked to Ethan's table. When I got there, all four guys were silent. I set the beers before each one of them, unable to meet any of their gazes. When I went to pull my hand back from setting the beer before Ethan, his snaked out and gently grabbed my fingers, lacing them through mine.

"Are you okay?" His other hand reached out and tipped my chin up.

I knew if I met his gaze I would cry, so I focused on his nose. "I'm okay," I repeated, almost to myself.

"Where does that douchebag live?" James asked in a steely growl. He never spoke. I had maybe heard him say three words in the handful of times I met him.

A weak smile graced my lips. "Let it go, guys. It's

over." Pulling my fingers from Ethan's grasp, I walked back to the kitchen.

Why had I thought divorcing Bryce would solve all of my problems? I should have known he wouldn't let me go until he was done with me.

Problem was, he'd told me once that I would only ever leave him in a body bag. At the time I wondered if it was a morbid joke. Now I prayed it wasn't true.

SEVEN

When Ethan came in with his boys, they normally stayed for a couple hours and left. But this time, when his friends left, he stayed and kept ordering bottled water every hour. I was still shaken from my run-in with Bryce, and when Mickey cut me at 2AM for my shift, Ethan wordlessly led me outside and we got on his bike. As I clung to him, driving home, my eyes darted around for that black sedan. How long would Bryce stay here? Surely he had to get back to work ... unless he'd asked his dad for a transfer to the Phoenix firm. The very thought made bile rise up in my throat.

Did he know I lived here above the garage with Ethan? Could he break in and...? I hadn't even realized we had reached home until Ethan stepped off the bike. We still hadn't talked; Ethan was good like that. He could pick up on my emotional shutdowns and he knew when he shouldn't push me or force me to say anything. Maybe he'd learned it living with his mom…

The very thought that Ethan was well equipped to deal with me because of his experience with his mother made depression settle into my bones.

By the time we reached the top of the stairs, I felt a mild panic at the thought of sleeping alone tonight.

"Can I lie with you?" I blurted out. "Just for tonight?"

When he turned to face me, his eyes were alight. "Of course."

I nodded. "I'll just change."

I had seen his door cracked open once and knew he had a big bed, not the twin that I had, and a more luxurious bathroom. So I popped into my room, pulled on my white silky sleep shorts and a tank top and brushed my teeth.

I'm not done with you.

I'm not done with you.

I'm not done with you.

When I padded down the hall and into Ethan's bedroom, he was lying shirtless, in basketball shorts, on the far left side of the bed. It was summer in

Arizona. No one slept fully clothed, I reminded myself.

Without a word, I slipped into his gray soft sheets and lay on the pillow.

My heart was hammering in my chest, because I was still scared of Bryce, or because I was in Ethan's bed. I wasn't sure.

"Sorry, I'm just a bit frazzled from earlier," I told him, embarrassed that a grown woman was afraid to sleep alone.

"Hailey." Ethan's voice was right by my ear.

"Yeah."

"If he ever touches you like that again, I'll kill him." His breath was hot on my neck.

I knew without a doubt that what Ethan said was the truth. I let exhaustion take me then and slept better than I had in years.

WHEN I WOKE UP, there was something soft and warm under my face. I snuggled into the warmth until I remembered I'd fallen asleep in Ethan's bed. My eyelids snapped open to find that I was lying on Ethan's chest, my mouth hovering just above his nipple. His hand was wrapped around my back, resting between my shoulder blades.

Panic rushed through me and I rolled off of him. I sat up and the motion stirred him awake.

He peeled his blue eyes open, and they combed for me like searchlights.

"Hey." He stretched casually, like we didn't just fucking snuggle the night away.

"Hey." I had no idea what to say.

Good morning, the last thing you said to me was that you were going to kill my ex if he ever touched me again and then I slept better than I had in years.

He sat up. "Want some eggs?"

I smirked. "Is that all you know how to make?"

"Yep."

Standing, I adjusted my tank top, which had ridden above my waist. Ethan King had yet to try my cooking.

"I'll make breakfast. Cooking is kinda my thing," I told him, and sauntered out of the room.

He grinned. "Alright, I'll take my insulin and have a shower."

Insulin. I'd forgotten for a moment that he was diabetic. He needed to take insulin before he ate … to prepare his body to deal with the sugars.

Looking at Ethan from the outside, you would never guess there was a single weakness in his body.

FORTY-FIVE MINUTES later I'd made a veggie egg quiche with a Bisquick crust. We'd just slept in bed together and now I was making him breakfast. *What is going on?*

He took one bite and looked at me with wide eyes. "You're telling me you could cook like this the entire time and I've been ordering pizza?"

Laughter pealed out of me. "Bake. I can bake. Anything in the oven I'm good at. Stove, not so much."

"Whatever, this needs to happen more often." He shoved another bite in his mouth. "Like ... can you make cookies and stuff?"

I was wearing a permanent grin. "Yes. Cookies, brownies, cake, anything in the oven."

"Well, my birthday is coming up and white chocolate macadamia nut cookies are my favorite. Just saying." He was grinning ear to ear as well.

Were we high? Was this what normal happy couples felt like? Not that we were a couple but ... this felt good. Too good to last.

"I'll keep that in mind." I winked.

I remembered this feeling all too well. Falling in love. I'd done it with Bryce and look where it got me.

"I've gotta go visit my brother up at Camp Verde prison today. Wanna come? The prison part is shit but driving up there through the mountains on the bike is beautiful." His tone was casual but his eyes said a different story.

I chuckled. "You want me to go to prison with you?"

His grin grew wider. "Yeah, why not? We can spend the day in Sedona, get our auras read or something."

That caused laughter to erupt out of me. Sedona was a tourist place known for its crystals, psychics, and vortex energy. It was also breathtakingly beautiful and twenty degrees cooler because it was in the mountains.

I had a ton of homework, but I might be able to slip away for a bit. Something told me if I did this, it would send Ethan a signal, a signal that I was open for ... dating or whatever this was.

I was so fucking torn I felt like I was being spilt open. Ethan's face was calm, but I had waited way too long for a normal person. This was officially "crazy girl with issues" length of time to respond.

"Sure. I'll shower and check my email. Then we can go?"

Fuck me. This guy was going to ruin me. I could feel it.

The pure smile that lit up his face when I said yes made my heart falter in my chest. Maybe we would ruin each other. Either way, there was no turning back now.

I was crushing on a felon and we were visiting his brother in prison.

Awesome.

My "friends" back in Beverly Hills would die if they knew, but I wasn't ashamed of where I came from and the people I'd grown up with.

After showering, I put on my new black lacy Target undies and cut-off jean shorts with a gray vintage t-shirt that said S.W.A.T. Another score from Goodwill. I was ready for this prison date.

I stepped out into the kitchen and Ethan's eye ran the length of my legs.

Heat crept up my face when his gaze landed on mine.

His voice was rough: "You look amazing."

I squirmed. "Thanks."

He rubbed the back of his neck in a nervous gesture. "But you can't wear that to prison. Do you have pants?"

My eyes widened. Stupid me! Showing leg when

I was about to go into a prison with a bunch of locked-up men who'd been deprived of sex.

"Yeah, I'll change."

After dying of embarrassment and changing into black leggings, I was ready to ride.

"Still look amazing?" I did a model pose with my long black leggings and Ethan's gaze hooded.

"Always."

It was a flirty joke, but his answer was dead serious. I had no reply for that.

"Let's ride." He gestured to his bike downstairs and I tried to get oxygen in my lungs. I forgot to breathe around Ethan. He affected me that much. I found myself wondering if I'd stayed at school with him and in this town if he and I would have dated.

WE HEADED out of the city on Ethan's bike, the hot wind whipping through my hair. There was something so soothing about being on the back of a motorcycle. You couldn't talk to each other, or look at your phone, you just ... breathed in nature, and if you were like me, let your mind go wild. Two times on the drive I'd sworn I had seen Bryce's white Range Rover. Me being alone with my thoughts for ninety minutes was interesting. Holding on to Ethan's chest, my legs spread and clenching his ass ... yeah you could say there was some sexual tension.

When the weather cooled off, and the red mountains of Sedona bloomed into view, Ethan took the offramp that led to the federal prison.

In L.A., I would never be visiting a friend in prison. This was so far removed from my Beverly Hills' lifestyle it was insane, and yet something about it felt fine. Ethan and I grew up in the hood, and unfortunately we didn't have the same opportunities as the rich kids. We had to fight and claw and beg and steal our way through life. I'd probably have gone a completely different route had my mom not passed away and I not gone to that private school.

Once off the freeway, it was a short ten-minute drive into a small parking lot off of Camp Verde Prison.

Ethan stepped off the bike and rolled his shoulders. "Ever visited someone in prison?"

I laughed. "Nope. This will be my first time."

"It's not as scary as you think. I'll protect you." He winked.

Even though he was kidding, butterflies took flight in my stomach and I wasn't sure if it was the sexy wink or the declaration that he'd protect me.

I stood to my full height then, which was nothing

compared to him. "I can protect myself," I declared jokingly, and puffed my chest for good measure.

Ethan's eyes went stormy, his face serious. "Ever shot a gun?"

Jesus.

"No." I played with the hem of my shirt.

He nodded. "I'll take you to the shooting range sometime. Show you how."

Again with those fucking butterflies. Ethan wanted to show me to shoot a gun because he was worried about Bryce. He'd never say it, but that's why he brought it up. I knew it. Was I capable of shooting someone? I didn't think so. Even my monster of an ex. But it was another excuse to spend time with Ethan, which I was enjoying.

"Okay."

"Okay." He held out his hand for me and I looked at it, a little confused.

"Best to make it look like we're together so the other guys don't think you're single and make a pass," he stated.

My eyes bugged out and I slipped my hand into his as his fingers laced through mine. Holy shit, the nervousness that rushed through my body was epic teenager level. I was holding a man's hand for Christ sake, no big deal, and you'd think I was at a Jonas

Brothers' concert with the way my heart was hammering.

After signing into the front and waiting a few minutes, we were patted down. A female officer spent a lot of time around my breast area and I wanted to punch her in the face, but then remembered this was her job and people probably snuck in drugs and crap.

Once we were cleared, we entered a larger room with a bunch of picnic tables in it. A male inmate sat behind each one. Ethan held my hand closely, his other arm tucked behind my back. We made our way all the way to the back where a giant of a man sat looking out a window.

"Scotty!" Ethan shouted, and the man turned.

Wow. I thought Ethan was bad boy sexy. Scotty was a fucking hot silver fox. He looked only about thirty-five, but was already over fifty-percent gray-haired. I thought Ethan was tatted up? This dude had not an inch of bare skin except for his face. He looked menacing, and yet familiar with those ice blue eyes and wide smile as he looked at his brother, who held on to me.

"Ethan!" Scotty stood and they embraced quickly before we all sat. A handful of guards paced the aisles as we settled in.

103

"This is my friend Hailey. We both went to Sunnyside together."

I waved, unsure if I would be able to shake his hand or not.

"It's nice to meet you, Hailey from Sunnyside." His brother's eyes twinkled and I was shocked at how much their baritone voices were similar.

"You too." My eyes flicked over to where a woman was crying while holding onto her son's hand.

"How's the shop?" Scotty leaned back and put his arms behind his head like we were at a Sunday brunch.

Ethan nodded. "Really good. Did you get my deposit into your commissary account?"

Scotty nodded. "Yes. Thank you, brother. Helps the days pass by smoother when you can have top ramen and Doritos."

I chuckled and Scotty winked at me.

Ethan's big brother leaned forward then, looking at bit more serious. "Mom said you haven't returned her calls for over six months."

I realized in that moment that Ethan and I were still holding hands, because it clamped down on mine for a split second before relaxing.

"I have nothing to say to her," Ethan grit out.

Wait, what? The mother that he nearly died trying to protect? They didn't talk?

Scotty's face fell. "Come on, man. Don't make her pay for her mistakes twice."

Ethan dropped my hand then and crossed his arms. "If she wants to stay with him, then she can, but I'll have no part in it."

Oh shit. It dawned on me then. I had completely assumed after Ethan beat the shit out of his dad that she left him.

As if reading my mind, Ethan looked over at me with stormy eyes. "Not everyone is strong enough to walk away."

Holy shit. This was huge. I no longer felt like the totally fucked-up dark and twisty one. Ethan had his own shit to deal with.

Scotty sighed. "Alright, well, when I get out, we're all going to have a party, okay? Mom, Dad, and you better be there."

Ethan just nodded curtly.

"Oh, when are you getting out?" I asked.

Scotty looked at me with a mischievous grin. "Six years, if I can stop kicking people's asses in here."

"And selling drugs," Ethan added.

Then they both laughed.

Alright, so the man knew his flaws and was

willing to be accountable to them. I could respect that. He had some loose morals and he was hot as fuck. Not as hot as Ethan, who had purity to him that Silver Fox didn't, but … I wasn't minding the view.

Hailey 2.0 checked guys out.

The next hour passed quickly. The talk turned light and we all shared funny stories. Scotty asked more about my schooling and told me he used to work at Mickey's too, as a bouncer. He was easy to talk to and generally pleasant, which was weird considering I'd expected a cold-blooded killer with an attitude or something. By the time the guards were asking us to leave, I realized that I had genuinely enjoyed my first prison visit experience.

"How often do you visit him?" I asked as we walked hand in hand out to his bike.

He shrugged. "Try to once a month. Sometimes it's once every few months when the shop gets busy."

I nodded.

He handed me my helmet. "Wanna grab lunch in town? I know a great place."

I shoved the helmet lightly into his chest. "If you promise to start wearing a helmet of your own."

His lips twitched. "Really? You're gonna starve

me until I submit to your will?" There was a sexy look in his eyes and I was liking it.

I nodded, crossing my arms. "Swear to start wearing a helmet and I'll go to lunch with you."

He licked his lips to wet them and looked me up and down. "Hailey Willows, the girl who got Ethan King to start wearing a helmet."

Laughter pealed out of me. "You must really want lunch."

His stormy blue gaze sharpened. "Something like that."

The air charged with particles or something, because the tension was so thick I could feel it as a tangible thing.

Shoving the helmet onto my head, I mumbled something about being hungry.

With a nod, we set off for our day in Sedona.

Over the next three hours we talked and laughed and walked up and down the strip of Sedona's downtown. We had an awesome lunch, where Ethan proceeded to wine and dine me with all of the local yummies. Then we had a laugh at the ice cream store when a lady with a thick accent said what sounded like "bitch" instead of peach. Next, we were just walking out of the aura shop when Ethan pulled out his picture they'd printed for him.

"Look at all that green? That means I'm totally going to be rich!" he explained, showing me his picture card.

I laughed, "No it's not. Green means intelligent and quick-witted." I pointed to the print under the picture.

He then scanned my red aura photo. "Damn, Hailey, you need to work on your anger." Reaching out, he tickled my side playfully and I grinned, moving closer to him naturally.

"Not angry. Passionate, see." I showed him the print under my photo.

Our eyes locked then and it's like all the air got sucked out of the space. People walked around us, but it's like they weren't there. If this were a movie, this would be when everything would go into slow motion and he would kiss me.

I wanted to.

My body gravitated towards him like a fucking magnet, but...

I wasn't ready.

He licked his lips as if in anticipation and I broke eye contact. "We should head home. I've got so much homework."

Fuck. I was so fucking broken I couldn't even be

normal with a guy I really liked. I wanted to cry at the thought.

I knew Ethan would never hurt me, but anxiety isn't rational.

"Yeah. Let's head back."

As we turned the corner to where he parked his bike, Ethan reached out and pulled me back.

"What—?" Before I could ask what was going on, he stepped forward and bent, inspecting his bike's tire, which was now flat.

When he looked up at me, his face was coated in anger. "Someone slashed my tires."

Bryce.

I knew it with a hundred-percent certainty.

That motherfucker wouldn't leave me alone, and now I'd pulled Ethan into it.

"I'M SO SORRY," I told Ethan again. He'd had to rent a car and arrange for one of his buddies to drive his bike back once the tires were fixed.

We were just coming into the front office at his shop and he turned to look at me with those piercing blue eyes. "You don't ever need to apologize to me, Hailey. Especially when you didn't do anything."

Geeze, he was so nice ... it made everything worse. I'd pulled this nice hot felon into my psycho life and now I didn't know what to do.

"Maybe the cops will see something on the CCTV," I offered.

"Maybe." He didn't sound convinced.

The moment the police had arrived and confirmed the tires had slash marks consistent with a knife, it looked like they were going to investigate. But when they asked why we were in town and Ethan had told him he was visiting his brother at the local prison, their gazes all turned judgmental. Like we ran with the wrong crowd and therefore deserved to have our tires slashed.

Fuckers.

They'd promised to look into the CCTV of the surrounding restaurants and give us a call. I didn't have the balls to mention Bryce and the fact that I might have seen his car as we were driving up. Ethan would just flip out, and the cops wouldn't have had anything to go on. But I could tell by the way Ethan watched his rearview mirror on the drive home that he suspected it.

Before I knew it, we were home and at the top of the stairs, ready to part ways and go to our separate rooms. Unless ... I'd just slept in his bed last night because I was scared, and I was still scared, but I didn't know what this was and I didn't want it to go too fast. Especially with a psycho ex to muddle a new relationship.

Ethan just looked at me with that innocent ice-blue gaze. "You wanna?" He pointed to his room. "I mean, if you sleep better that way, I'm cool," he mumbled.

I did. I'd had the best night's sleep in seven years in his bed, but...

"I think I'll be okay." I rubbed my arms and stared at the floor.

Ethan's hand snaked out and tilted my chin up to meet his eyes.

"Even though we had a bump in the road, I still had an amazing day with you."

Fuck. My heart knocked into my chest and I wanted to lean into him, to press my body against his and let the warmth of his skin melt into mine. I wanted to feel his rock hard chest against my body—I wanted to fuck him. I hadn't wanted to have sex in years. I did it monthly out of obligation to Bryce, and I would lay there moving with the same rocking motion, thinking about what I would make for dinner, faking an orgasm every other time so he wouldn't get mad. I'd thought my vagina had shriveled up and died, and now with Ethan's hand on my chin I wanted to reach into his pants and see what we were dealing with.

I let out the breath I was holding and stepped back. "I had an amazing day too. Night." I spun and hightailed it out of there before I started to hump his leg.

I was *definitely* buying a vibrator tonight.

Ethan King just did it for me. Merely looking at him made everything in my body ramp up a notch, and when we touched it was ten times more. I couldn't imagine what would happen if I kissed him. I was liable to explode.

Sometimes a girl needed to explode.

EIGHT

The next month passed by in a blur of school and work and work and school. When I wasn't doing that, I was doing homework, and in the rare hours of doing nothing I was with Ethan or Angela. Angela would bring her adorable son over to play, while Ethan would BBQ for us, or Ethan would call me out to the living room, where I'd make popcorn and we'd watch a movie together.

I'd finally ordered that vibrator to try and quell the sexual tension between Ethan and I, but that was a fucking disaster. For starters, Ethan didn't notice my name on the box and opened the package. Then he'd re-taped it and set it in front of my door. But by the red in his cheeks, and adjusting of his pants the next time he saw me, I knew he'd seen it. When I'd tried to use it, all I thought about was screwing Ethan's brains out. I definitely needed therapy. I wanted to have sex with him but was too scared— what a shit show. The one glimmer of hope over the past month was that Bryce had gone radio silent. I was hoping that meant he was back in L.A., where he belonged. Probably making someone else's life hell.

It was hotter than the devil's armpit outside. I was just riding my bike home from the light rail stop, sweat dripping from every pore of my skin, when I saw Ethan taking a new motorcycle off a trailer. He rolled it into his shop as I pulled up and wheeled my bike inside.

Summer in AZ meant wearing as little of clothes as possible and I was doing just that. A neon crop top I'd scored at Target and Daisy Dukes with flip-flops. The second I was done with nursing school, I changed from those thick hot scrubs in the school bathroom.

Ethan had stopped moving the bike, as it was midway down the ramp, and now was raking his gaze up and down my body.

Fuck me. He wasn't subtle about it either.

I didn't know how much more I could take of this. Living with this tattooed god who never wore a shirt and didn't have an ounce of fat on his body ... it was torture. My heart and my head needed to have a powwow and come to terms. Assuming Ethan would even want to hook up with me. Though the growing bulge in his pants confirmed he'd probably be down.

A slow grin crept across my face as I walked over to the small shop fridge and grabbed an ice cold Gatorade. After chugging half the thing, Ethan's deep voice sounded right behind me.

"Would you ever get on one of these?"

I spun around, a lump in my throat. Sweat made a slow trickle down his eight pack before changing directions as it diverted to his V-shape and into the motherland.

"Yeah? What?"

Where was I? What year was it? Do me now, Ethan King.

He grinned. "If I fixed up this bike for you, would you ever want to learn to ride?" He gestured to the clunker that just got brought in.

Ohhh, right. I shook my head. "Umm, eighty miles an hour on the 101? Probably not. Maybe a Vespa though. Those are cute. A blue one." I smiled.

He looked horrified. "A Vespa? There is no way I'm letting you ever drive a Vespa."

I shrugged. "I don't mind the light rail and my bike."

His brow furrowed. "It's really hot out though, and with a motorcycle you could be home in ten minutes versus the forty-five it takes you now."

I genuinely felt safe on Ethan's motorcycle when he was driving, but didn't think driving one myself was my thing. A pang of sadness ripped through me then. I missed my Audi.

I groaned. "I should have fought harder for my Audi in the divorce."

Ethan froze. It was the first time I'd ever talked about my divorce; it just slipped out.

"You had an Audi?"

I cringed a little and then nodded. "A white TT. Bryce bought it for me."

His mouth formed a grimacing line. "Of course he did."

Yeah, Ethan didn't like Bryce one bit.

"I'll save up and get a car eventually. Don't worry about me." I went to move past him, but he snaked out and grabbed my arm gently.

The mere gentle touch of his fingers on my wrist sent heat traveling down my spine. Looking up, we locked eyes.

"I do worry."

I do worry. For some reason those words had emotions forming a bump in my throat.

I'd never had someone who worried about me. Not in a long time. Bryce was possessive but never worried about my safety or my health, he just wanted to control my schedule. This was different.

I kept his gaze. "I'm fine. I promise."

He sighed, releasing my wrist.

"I've got studying to do," I mumbled, and ran upstairs with my backpack slung around my shoulder. Living with Ethan was making it harder and harder to resist him. But I'd just gotten out of a toxic and abusive long relationship; I wasn't ready to start anew. And I didn't want to fuck up my one shot with Ethan King by bringing all of my baggage on board. Bryce was the first and only guy I'd ever slept with. The third guy I'd kissed. And my everything, every day, for the past seven years. I didn't even know how to flirt or what kissing another guy would be like.

Maybe I needed a trial run on some loser from Mickey's before trying to dive in with the perfect and delectable Ethan. What if I went to kiss a guy and had some traumatic flashback and started to cry or something fucked up? That would ruin anything Ethan and I had been building towards. He would run for the hills. Broken goods, do not purchase.

Fuck.

I had tonight off...

Picking up my phone, I shot Angela a text before I got the nerve to back out.

I want to go out dancing tonight, get hammered and make out with some random guy.

Her reply was instant. **Bitch it's on. I'll get a sitter.**

I grinned. This was just what I needed. Some fling to get my rusty pipes moving and make sure I wasn't going to fall to pieces if another man touched me. Tonight was guinea pig night.

Flipping open my laptop, I scrolled my messages and an email popped up, sending my heart jumping into my throat.

(Subject: Visa-Thank you for your payment.)

It was from my credit card, the one with the mondo balance that I'd used to pay for my divorce and escape Bryce. The one which I didn't pay for another two weeks. Dread seeped into my gut as I opened the message.

Paid in full.

Current open line of credit $7,000.

No. He didn't? He couldn't have found out about my secret card, could he? But who else would pay it? That motherfucker went radio silent for a month and then he paid off my card?! He was trying to buy me back. It's the same thing his parents did with him and the only way he knew how to deal with love.

With shaking hands, I dialed the credit card company. Maybe this was a misunderstanding. After putting in my card number and screaming, "Human being, sales representative!" to the robot bitch, I got a human.

"Hello and thank you—"

"I need you to tell me who paid off my balance," I said in a rush.

"Okay, I just need to let you know that this call is recorded and—"

"I know, that's fine. Please, it's urgent," I told the clueless lady with a Texas accent.

"Okay..." She tapped away on her computer and I held my breath. "Based on the card number you put in when you called, it looks like your balance was just paid a few hours ago via..." She paused: "Cash drop off at our Phoenix location."

Motherfucker. "Who did it?" I growled.

"Excuse me?" The woman sounded distraught. "Didn't you? You're the sole card holder, Ma'am."

Breathe. Just fucking breathe.

"Actually, that's the issue. I didn't. My ex-husband did, without my permission, and I need you to return the funds."

She chuckled. "Return the payment? Honey, all my ex-husband gave me was a rash and a mountain of debt."

Eww.

"Look, can I speak to your supervisor? I really need this returned. It's complicated."

She paused.

"Oh, alright. I'll ask him what's possible. Please hold." Her voice held a little more compassion then.

I paced my room, wearing foot marks into the area rug I'd gotten in the clearance aisle at Wal-Mart. Bryce wouldn't stop, he would do this until I went back to him. At work, they called him the Bird Dog. He would run after clients and not let up until he brought one back.

Alive or dead.

"Hi, this is Daniel, the supervisor over here at—"

"Can you please return my payment?" I was getting really annoyed with this overly polite bull-shit. No one loved working customer service that much, and didn't they know my life was falling apart?

"Ma'am, I'm sorry, if it were a wire transfer or check I could. This was paid in cash, so who would I return it to but you?"

Fuck.

Defeat crept into my very bones then. Bryce knew what he was doing.

"Okay ... thank you." I hung up and fell face-first into my bed, screaming in frustration into my pillow.

I wrestled with what to do about the situation over the next hour as I got ready for my night out with Angela. Did I call Bryce? Tell him to fuck off? Tell Ethan he paid off my credit card? Tell the police he was the nicest stalker in the world paying off my shit?

Everything felt hopeless and wouldn't heed the results I wanted. Calling Bryce would only give him what he wanted, which was contact with me. Telling Ethan would only enrage him. Calling the police for something like this was a joke.

I was going to go out tonight, get completely smashed, and forget that this shit show had ever happened. After showering, I looked at my two options for dresses. Option one, a super adorable pink sundress that was flowy and would look sexy with black heels. Option two, a total fuck-me-from-behind black tight number with mesh cutouts on the sides.

Ethan's Kings club meeting was tonight. He would totally be out there watching me as I walked to leave...

With that in mind, I chose option two.

Bryce would have thrown me in the closet and tossed away the key if I ever wore something this provocative. After trying it on in the store, I'd put it back, but Angela had encouraged me to buy it.

"Honey, trust me, one day you will pop out three kids and your boobs will be at your knees and you will regret never wearing a dress like this," she'd said.

She was right. Hailey 2.0 liked her body and wanted to show it off once in a while. Especially when Ethan was around to see it.

After packing my booty into the size four dress, I curled my hair and put on make-up. Bryce had never let me get to a size six. Any time I gained weight he would repeatedly mention going to the gym and not eating carbs. It was only now that I looked at the dress size number, which was a bit snug since I'd last tried it on, that I realized he'd probably given me an eating disorder. I'd been eating a bit more carefree with Ethan and put on a healthy five pounds; that would have never happened in L.A., not without consequences. Each time I realized a part of myself that Bryce had tainted, it made me horribly sad. Taking a deep breath, I shook it off, choosing to focus on the good.

Holy shit, I was going out with a girlfriend and Bryce wasn't there to shoot daggers at me if I said something stupid or danced funny or talked to another guy. This was going to be epic!

When Angela texted me that she was getting into an Uber and on her way to pick me up, I made my way out of my room. A group of male voices floated up from the shop room floor where their "meeting" was being held. Their meetings consisted of drinking beer—though I noticed Ethan never seemed to drink too much—and talking shit about other people and each other. Who had a nicer bike, who was more buff, who fucked the most girls blah, blah, blah. I would listen to their chats waft up over the staircase and chuckle sometimes. Men were so predictable. Motorcycles, working out, and sex was about all they cared about.

The second my black stiletto heel stepped onto the top step, every single voice hushed. My gaze flicked to the group of guys, all standing around their bikes, with a beer in one hand, and some with a cigarette in the other.

"Damn, baby," Nick called from down below and cat-call whistled at me. Ethan *thwopped* him on the back of the head.

"Don't talk to her like that," he growled.

Nick scowled at Ethan but kept his mouth shut while I tried to suppress a grin. There were ten guys in the crew but I really only knew Ethan, Nick, James, and Sebastian. The others didn't work at the shop or stop by if it wasn't a meeting night.

"Going out?" Ethan's voice was low and growly as his eyes raked down my dress; his Adam's apple bobbed as he gave a hard swallow.

I smiled innocently, liking the effect my dress was having on him. Even though he was in a t-shirt and jeans, he had the same effect on me. Just looking as his huge tattooed biceps made me want to wrap my thighs around him.

I'd reached the base of the stairs. "Going dancing with Angela."

He took a swig of his beer. "Need a ride?"

I shook my head. "We're sharing an Uber."

He nodded. "Need a chaperone?" A grin pulled at his lips and a few of his friends chuckled.

Now it was my turn to smile. I pretended to think about it. "Nah, I feel like being bad tonight. Chaperone might cramp my style."

I'd never forget the fire that lit up his blue eyes, the way his nostrils flared and his lips puckered outward. His friends erupted into a chorus of "Ohh-hhh," and I walked right past him and outside to the waiting car.

I hadn't meant to, but I was playing hard to get with Ethan, leading him on. I just hoped I was leading him somewhere I was capable of going. I guess we would see tonight. It was guinea pig night. Time to see just how fucked up single Hailey 2.0 was at dating.

THE MUSIC WAS loud and I was two stiff drinks in. Enough to feel good but not enough to be totally sloppy. I was grinding up on a hot guy and everything seemed to be going well. Except it wasn't. The hot guy I was grinding on wasn't Ethan. He wasn't Bryce either, which was a nice change, but it was like my body was repelled by this beautiful man before me because it was wondering why the fuck we weren't grinding on Ethan.

I. Needed. Therapy. NOW. What the hell was I doing? This was one of the stupid things that fucked up chicks did. They went out to see how broken they were so that they could hopefully be fixed for a new guy? What the hell was wrong with me? The guy's hands had been respectfully on my lower back for the last three songs, but now they started to migrate down towards my ass.

But what if I went to kiss Ethan and something majorly wild happened to ruin it? I hadn't kissed a nice guy in seven years.

"Kiss me!" I shouted into the dude's ear, realizing now that two drinks were enough to make me sloppy. Because this was the stupidest thing I'd ever done.

He pulled his head back and desire flashed in his gaze. Boy was pretty. Pre-med at ASU with mani-cured eyebrows. I mean, he could be gay he was that pretty. I just wanted to pick someone opposite of Ethan and I ended up picking Bryce 2.0.

Fuck.

As he leaned in to kiss me, I braced for impact. My whole body froze and I winced.

This isn't right—this isn't how it should be—I'm not ready.

Before he could get to my lips, I panicked and took both of my palms, planting them on his chest and giving a big shove. He flew backward, eyes wide, and a few people turned to stare at us.

He looked at me incredulously. "What the fuck is wrong with you?"

I'm broken.

I burst from the dance floor mumbling an apology and over to the bar, where I ordered two shots of tequila. Tequila was my go-to if I wanted to erase parts of my memory and forget what it was like to feel pain. Tequila and I were frenemies.

I charged both shots to my newly-paid-off credit card just to spite Bryce, or myself, I couldn't tell. Just as I was ordering a third, Angela came up behind me.

"Hey, you okay? I saw you push that dude."

I tipped the bartender a hundred dollars on the credit card, and now I was sure I was just screwing myself over and not Bryce.

"I'm not ready," I told Angela, and took back the third shot. It made a slow burn all the way down my throat.

Angela's mouth made an O-shape as she dragged me from the bar to a quieter part of the club.

"Wanna go home?" she screamed over the music.

I frowned, feeling the three shots of tequila burn though my stomach and right into my soul. "Not ready for that either."

Angela knew Bryce was abusive, but I didn't go into detail. Same with Ethan. I didn't tell either of them anything that would make them look on me with any more pity.

"Dance with me, then!" Angela smiled, pulling me onto the dance floor and holding my arms up in the air, twirling beneath them.

I tipped my head back and laughed. Angela was what I needed. Not some new guy, or an old guy, or any guy. I just needed to have fun with my friend. We danced for a bit before I started to feel dizzy and fell over.

Angela gave me a mom look. "How many shots did you take?"

I held up four fingers, but then pulled one down before getting confused and putting it up again. Angela grinned. "Okay, beautiful, it's time to go home. Tequila is how I got pregnant. We don't want none of that for you."

I just nodded, too far in my dizzy world to put up an argument. When Angela called the Uber and gave the driver her address, I corrected her. "No, I want to see Ethan," I mumbled. Thinking of that big tattooed teddy bear made me feel safe. I knew he would stay up and worry about me if I didn't come home or text him, and I wanted to see him. I had to tell him something.

She raised an eyebrow. "You sure?"

I nodded. "Five hundred-percent." My words

were slurred so I threw in a military salute for good measure.

Ten minutes later we were pulling up to the shop. A shirtless Ethan stood outside with his hands in his pockets.

"I texted him," Angela told me.

I was so tired, I just wanted to curl up on Ethan's chest and sleep forever. But I couldn't because that's all I'd ever be ready for. I'd never be able to take it, whatever this was, to the next level. I wasn't ready and he'd get sick of waiting.

When Ethan opened my side of the Uber, I stumbled out and nearly face-planted. He caught me, his hands wrapping around my hips to steady me.

"Whoa." His voice was deep and husky.

"She's a bit ... keep an eye on her. I've gotta go relieve my kid's sitter." Angela cleared her throat.

"I will. Thank you, Angela." Ethan shut the door and the Uber drove off.

"Love you, Ang!" I shouted as the car drove off, laughter bubbling up in my chest.

"Okay, Hailey, let's get you to bed." He led me into the shop and locked the doors behind him.

"Do you feel sick? Do you want some water?" he asked as I stumbled my way through the shop floor, stepping over tools and wheels and bike parts. I stopped suddenly and spun around to face him.

"Don't do that, okay." I put my hand out on his chest. "Don't be so nice to me."

He frowned. "Why wouldn't I be nice to you?"

My hand was still on his chest and my emotions were pinging inside of me like a pinball machine. "I tried to kiss another guy tonight. To see if I was ready." His eyes flashed cobalt blue, the veins in his neck protruding. "And when he got close enough, I froze like a rabbit about to be eaten by her prey."

A whimper escaped me and Ethan's hand came up to lace through mine.

"He broke me, Ethan. He broke me for every other guy." Tears streamed down my face as the tequila danced around my body like a squirrel at a rave. I was going to regret this shit tomorrow.

Ethan stepped closer to me, pressing his body against mine. He bent into a squat and hooked his arms under me, pulling me to his chest. My heels slipped off as he carried me up the stairs.

"You're not broken, you just haven't finished putting yourself back together yet." His breath tickled my neck as I snuggled closer to his chest.

I spoke my deepest fear aloud. "What if I can't? What if his power over me is too strong?"

Ethan's fingers came up to stroke my forehead as he pulled hair away from my face. "You're the one with all the power. You just haven't realized it yet."

Sleep was pulling at my limbs, and the spins had me inside of a washing machine. "What if it takes too long?" I mumbled. "And by then you won't want me anymore."

Whoa, did I say that out loud? I was totally assuming he wanted me in the first place. *Fuck you, tequila, you are not being nice right now.*

"I'm a patient man," he whispered against my ear, and that was the last thing I remembered before sleep took me.

THE MORNING SUNLIGHT cast warmth across my face. I peeled my eyes open and a throbbing drum started to knock at the base of my skull and I winced.

Moaning, I rolled over and took stock of my surroundings. I was in Ethan's room, lying in his bed. Glancing down I noticed I was wearing one of his t-shirts. My dress was gone but I was still wearing my bra and undies underneath. Oh God. Did he undress me? Color flooded my cheeks as I remembered what

I'd said to him last night. Did I really tell him I was broken and basically ask him to wait for me?

Kill me now.

I heard rustling in the kitchen and was halfway tempted to crawl back under the covers and never leave this room—ever.

But my throat was so dry it felt like sandpaper. I had to face this sometime. I was going to pull on my big girl panties and just do it now.

After going pee, I brushed my teeth. Ethan had left a brand new toothbrush on the counter, still in the wrapper—because he was fucking thoughtful like that. Because he was the kind of guy that girls were dying to marry and I was trying to push him away because I had issues.

After allowing myself a good full seven minutes to feel sorry for myself, I opened the door and waltzed out into the kitchen like I had my shit together.

I looked like a hooker who'd woken up in a motel room and was now trying to get her money before she left. But that was okay. Ethan had seen me at my worst. A little mascara under my eyes wasn't going to scare him off if last night didn't.

He was standing beside the sink shaking his protein shake, something he made after a workout.

When he heard me approach, he looked up at me and I just stood there a moment, watching him. Shirtless, sweating, and shaking this bottle so hard it caused all of his muscles to tighten. My thighs clenched and I cleared my throat.

"Wow. So, can we just pretend last night didn't happen?" I laughed nervously before wincing at how loud my fucking voice was.

A half smirk lit up his face. "Sure thing."

I sighed in relief. He wasn't going to mention anything, we could forget it happened and all would be well.

"Just one thing," he said, and popped the top of his protein shake.

I braced myself for whatever he was going to say.

"You threw up all over your dress, that's why you're in my shirt."

Fuck.

I bit my lip trying to disappear. I needed Harry Potter to toss me under his invisibility cloak so I could slink off to my bedroom in shame.

I just nodded.

He stepped closer to me and looked down at my bare legs. "I just didn't want you to think I would ever undress you without your permission."

My heart beat so loudly then I felt like it had jumped into my head and taken residence there.

"Right," I whispered. Ethan's soul was too pure for this world.

With a nod he started for his bedroom. "I'm going to shower."

Of course you are. You're going to get naked and rub soap all over and I'm not going to think about it.

"Hey, Ethan...?" I called out after him.

When he turned to look at me, there was something in his gaze ... compassion? Pity? I couldn't tell.

"Thanks for taking care of me." I ran my fingers through my tangled hair. "I ... ugh ... got married at eighteen so..." I let that sentence linger because what the hell was I doing? I didn't know, I just wanted to fix things.

He nodded. "So your young wild years were taken from you?" he guessed.

I guessed they were; I guessed last night was the twenty-first birthday I never had.

I just nodded.

Ethan shrugged. "No worries. I'm just glad you got home safely."

Then he slipped into his room and I was left feeling like shit. Something had started between Ethan and I, whether I wanted it to or not, and I was messing it up by holding back. I knew that. It was like watching a train crash; I couldn't stop it. I hadn't expected to meet someone so soon after Bryce, and mending my heart while also opening to a new person ... wasn't working. Shuffling my feet, I sulked all the way back to my bedroom. I had class in two hours, then work. Life didn't stop for hangovers and bad choices. I was going to have to strap those big girl panties on and deal with it.

NINE

I could barely stomach any breakfast, and class was hard to sit through. I just kept thinking of Ethan carrying me up those stairs, whispering into my neck that he'd wait for me to figure my shit out. *Maybe I shouldn't be living with him. Maybe I should hire a hit man and take out Bryce.* I laughed at that thought. Bryce made the darkest parts of me reveal itself. I couldn't really ever kill him. Not like that. I just wanted him to go away, I wanted to move on, and I couldn't do that with the threat of him hanging over me and Ethan.

My mind gnawed all day at my problems until I finally got to work and made myself busy tending the bar. Mickey was starting to teach me all the drinks and how to stock everything for when we were busy and needed two bartenders. It was 1AM and I was pretty sure I would be cut soon. Mick knew I had class in the morning and tried to cut me early on those days. I'd Ubered here, and planned to do the same going home. Now that I was making decent money, I had a good monthly budget going, with cash set aside for late-night Ubers. Ethan always offered to drive me, and I usually took him up on it, but not tonight. Tonight, I was too ashamed to even look at him. I'd snuck off to work without seeing him so I didn't have to decline his offer.

"Hailey, you're cut!" Mickey yelled over the music.

I nodded, and wiped down my station before going to the back room to clock out. I decided to shoot Ethan a text and tell him I was Ubering home in case he was worrying.

When I opened my phone I saw that a text from him was waiting.

I'm at Nick's down the street, text me when you're off and I'll drive you home.

I sighed. He was a good friend. He cared. And that's just what I needed right now.

I'm off now. I can just call an Uber if you're home.

His reply was instant.

On my way.

Well, saving six dollars wasn't the worst thing in the world, and if Ethan was willing to look past last night, then hopefully we could pretend it didn't happen.

Nick's was only a five-minute drive away. I threw my bag over my shoulder and headed outside to wait for him. The craziest thing about living in the desert was how hot it got even in the middle of the night. It was 1 AM and probably ninety-five degrees out. Heat blasted my face as I stared out at the passing cars.

Then a hand clamped over my mouth and started dragging me backwards.

"You little whore," Bryce growled in my ear.

Panic ripped through me as he dragged me into the alley between Mickey's and the Laundromat. I was so terrified, and it was happening so quickly, that I couldn't think straight. By the time my wits came back to me, he had me pinned against the brick wall, hand over my throat, with my legs spread and his thigh between them.

"I saw you dancing last night. Wearing that

dress. Trying to get fucked!" His light blond hair and ice-blue eyes made him look demonic with the way shadows cast across his face from the streetlamp. I'd never seen him so enraged.

"You want me to fuck you? Is that what it will take to bring you home?" His hand trailed down my stomach and I froze, petrified. I'd always envisioned being a badass fighter when put in this type of position, but instead of lashing out with all of the rage I'd built up towards Bryce, my body just shut down and I froze. The only thing I could focus on was breathing.

Just breathe.

I whimpered and he lessened his hold on my throat. "I want you to move out of that tattooed scumbag's house and come home to me, understand?"

Breathe.

Just then I heard the roar of a motorcycle.

Ethan.

"No. It's ... over," I got out before he clamped down harder, making black spots dance at the edges of my vision.

"It's over when I say it's over. You took a fucking vow. You promised to love me no matter what. You lying. Little. Bitch." He growled and moved his hand to unbutton my jeans.

Oh my God. This was my worst nightmare, but I couldn't let him win. I had to stay strong.

"I ... can't ... love ... a monster," I rasped, and then a blur streaked before my vision, taking Bryce down to the ground.

Bryce was knocked to his side and the pressure lifted off my throat. Gasping, I took painful lungfuls of precious air. Ethan dropped down onto his knees, straddling Bryce and pinning him to the asphalt. He raised his arms and landed blow after blow into Bryce's face. Each smack was delivered with such force, I knew immediately that Ethan was strong enough to kill him. All Bryce could do was raise his arms and try to protect himself, and if I stood there and did nothing Ethan would punch him into a coma, or worse. A very small part of me wanted to let him. Then it would be over, I would be free.

But I couldn't let Ethan go to jail for me. A previous felon beating the life out of a rich boy from L.A? It wouldn't bode well with the judge.

"Ethan, stop!" I surged forward, and with a hard shove knocked him off of Bryce.

Ethan jumped up to his feet, complete and utter

rage coursing through him as he stepped protectively in front of me.

Bryce skidded backward before standing, lip gushing blood, nose bleeding, and a rapidly swelling eye. I prayed by morning he would look like a sharpei puppy.

"If you ever touch her again, I'll kill you," Ethan ground out, body shaking with adrenaline.

"Not if you're in jail, you piece of shit!" Bryce held his chin high. "You just assaulted me!"

Fuck.

"Mickey has cameras on this alley," I lied. "The cops will see that you attacked me first and he was only protecting me." Mickey couldn't afford cameras, but I was a good bluffer. I'd been lying to Bryce for years.

Love you too, babe.

Of course I want a date night.

Nothing wrong, I'm just tired.

Fear flashed in his gaze for the first time in forever.

"Game over, motherfucker. Go back to L.A. and don't ever look for her again," Ethan stated.

I heard the unmistakable click of a gun. My eyes flicked down to Ethan's side, where he was holding his firearm loosely, finger on the trigger. It was adding power to his threat. Ethan meant every word he said, and part of me wanted him to just end it. Wipe Bryce from the face of the earth so he couldn't hurt anyone ever again.

Bryce looked like he was ready to catch fire, he was so livid. His nostrils flared as blood dripped in a slow trickle from his lip and nose. He could now only see out of one eye.

With heaving breaths, he walked past us, stopping to look right in Ethan's face. "She'll never love anyone like she loves me." Bryce spat at Ethan's feet and then left the alley in a huff.

All the adrenaline had been keeping me upright, but now that the threat had passed, my knees gave out and I fell to the concrete, panting.

"Oh my God!" I wept, my hand shaking as sobs racked my body. "Oh my God, oh my God." I couldn't stop. *He almost raped me. Killed me.* God knows what his plans were.

I was having a heart attack. I couldn't breathe. I was going to die right here in the alley at twenty-two years old. Ethan knelt next to me and placed a light hand on my back, which I shied away from before realizing it was just him.

"Are you okay?" His voice shook, and then he

must have realized he'd asked a stupid question. "Do you need a doctor?" he amended.

I just shook my head, trying to get my heart to slow down, trying not to think about how close he'd been to unbuttoning my jeans and choking me to death.

"Let's go to the police. File a report." He stood, pulling me up with him. Feeling his strong hands around my upper arms made me feel safe.

I am safe, I told myself to try and calm my nervous system.

I shook my head. "You have a previous felony on record and your knuckles are bleeding. When they go to question him and see his face, it will only get you in trouble."

Anger pulled at Ethan's features; his brows drew together and he grimaced. "I don't fucking care. That psycho needs to be behind bars. Even if I'm there with him."

In that moment I realized Ethan cared for me. Not just a mild crush, no, this was some deep shit that we'd both fallen into.

I whimpered. "Don't say that." Stepping forward, I clung to his arm. "I ... need you. Just take me home. Please."

I needed Ethan King like I needed air. He was my life vest when Bryce kept trying to drown me.

Ethan sighed, trying to control his own breathing. He was quiet for a long beat before he nodded. "Fine. But next time I'm killing him, consequences be dammed."

This right here was the reason I never should have moved in with Ethan. I'd dragged him into my life and now he was willing to go to jail for me. Some great influence I was. I ruined people's lives. Like a wrecking ball, I'd come in and thrown Ethan's world into chaos.

When we got back to his house, he just stood there in his kitchen, staring at the red ring of bruises that were now turning purple around my neck. It hung there like a necklace. A reminder that Bryce would try to own me at all costs.

"I... know you don't want to talk about your past. But I have to know. Has he done this before?" Ethan's voice could cut glass; his teeth clenched so tightly I thought they might break.

My gaze fell to his bleeding knuckles. He'd jumped on Bryce like a silverback gorilla and would have pounded the life out of him if I'd let him.

Maybe I should have...

"Not this bad," was all I could bring myself to say.

Ethan's chest rose and fell as he seemingly tried to control his breathing. I knew he was probably reliving some of what happened with his own father and I felt awful about that. He was quiet for a long minute.

"I'm tired. I'm gonna take a quick shower and then get some sleep. Would you please stay in my bed tonight? So I can make sure you're safe?"

My throat tightened, because he knew just what I needed. He wasn't going to make me go into more detail, and he knew I would be scared to sleep alone. He was so in-tune with me.

I just nodded.

That night I slept in Ethan's bed, again. It was the only real place I could get decent sleep anymore. Once again, we fell asleep on our own sides of the bed but I woke up in his arms. We were like fucking magnets that gravitated towards each other and I wasn't sure I could resist him much longer.

I kept thinking about last night, replaying it over and over in my head. I'd been so helpless, I should have head-butted Bryce or kicked him in the balls, but instead I'd just frozen in fear. What would have happened if Ethan hadn't shown up? I shivered to think about it. I'd never seen Bryce like that. I mean, I'd always thought he was capable of some pretty sinister things but ... not that.

"I'll make us breakfast," he declared, and stroked a light finger across my arm. It was a simple gesture of affection, but it had heat pooling between my legs. I wanted this man so badly, but fear kept me from acting on what my body kept begging for.

After cleaning up, I walked out to see Ethan scrambling eggs.

"I'd like to take you to the firing range. Teach you to shoot my gun," he casually blurted out.

Silence.

More silence.

All the silence.

Ethan probably now rightly suspected Bryce was more dangerous than I had initially let on. This was the time to open up and tell him my story. Tell him all of the horrible things that monster did to me over the course of our marriage, which I was now seeing I was manipulated into.

If we go off to college without being married, some other guy will steal you from me.

No they won't, I'd tried to reassure him.

Don't you want to prove your love to me? Don't you love me?

Then he'd taken college from me:

If you're always in classes, you can't be home to work on our marriage. Aren't I important to you?

But the scariest fucking thing he'd ever done was throw out my birth control.

He'd known things were bad between us, that I might leave, and he'd wanted to trap me with a baby.

Fuck that.

I'd gone right to Planned Parenthood and paid cash for the Depo shot.

"Hailey?" Ethan's face was shrouded with concern.

"Shooting range! Sounds fun."

I wasn't ready to tell Ethan my story. Not yet, and maybe not ever. Some things just shouldn't be relived. I wanted to enjoy the way he looked at me a little bit longer.

ETHAN'S ARMS were wrapped around me, his chest pressed against my back as he adjusted my grip on the pistol.

"Never point a gun at someone or something unless you are prepared to shoot them and kill them."

My heart was thumping against my chest, partly because he was talking about shooting people and partly because his crotch was pressed against my ass ... and I liked it.

Focus.

"Got it," I squeaked.

He placed noise-canceling headphones over my ears. "Take a deep breath, aim, and when you're ready, shoot."

I could hear him, just muffled. I was a little sad when he stepped away from me, taking his body heat with him.

He'd already taught me about the safety, which was now off, so all that was left to do ... was shoot.

Could I kill someone? Wasn't that why we were here? To teach me to defend myself in the event I was attacked or...

Bryce.

I'm not done with you yet.

I pulled back the trigger and the gun bucked back with power as the bullet shot out with such force it kicked my hand a little.

Adrenaline rushed through me as I stared at the target to see the very upper right corner had been hit.

"Great job," Ethan said from behind me, but his voice was deep and slurred. I thought it might be the earmuffs, so I took them off and turned around, setting the gun down on the counter like he'd taught me. When I looked up at him, I knew immediately that something was wrong. He was sitting in the chair against the wall, sweaty, pale, and staring off into the distance.

"You okay?"

He shook his head slowly, then went to stand and swayed a little on his feet. "I ... feel sick. Out ... of it. Blood ... sugar." He started to fall forward and I caught him. It was like catching a fucking bag of cement. His head crashed into my chest and we both went down together. I fell backward, allowing my body to break his fall. He was completely passed out. Panic ripped through me. I was only a nursing student for all of two months, but immediately I knew this had to be an issue with his diabetes.

"Call 911!" I shouted to the man who'd checked us in and was about twenty feet away staring at his computer screen, oblivious. His head snapped to our direction and shock lit up his features. "He's diabetic!" I shouted then, because I didn't want the man to think I'd shot Ethan.

Rolling Ethan over took every ounce of strength I had. I made sure he was breathing in case it was a heart attack or something more sinister.

He was.

I remembered seeing him tuck a black zipper pouch into his backpack before we left. I thought it was his blood glucose meter, which I'd seen him use a few times after we ate meals together.

Pulling the pouch out, I opened it. There was the meter, the poker thingy, and the strips. I was a nurse, I told myself. I could poke him and do this. He was either too high and needed insulin, or too low and needed glucose. If I guessed and stabbed him with his insulin pen, I could bring him even lower.

With shaky hands, I held the poker over his finger and pushed the button. Pulling it back, a droplet of blood escaped his fingertip; my heart pinched when I saw all the prick marks along his fingertips from the constant poking. He hid his disease well. I'd only ever seen him use it once or twice. By the time I loaded the strip and squeezed a drop of blood onto it, the man was standing before us on his cell phone.

"Is he breathing?" the man asked.

I nodded. And when the meter reading came, I almost fainted.

Twenty-seven.

That was low. Too low.

"Give me that!" I reached out and grabbed the phone from the man.

"He's a diabetic and his blood glucose meter says twenty-seven," I mumbled into the phone.

How did you get orange juice down someone's throat who was passed out?

"Okay, that's too low," a women's voice, strong and steady, came over the line. "I have an ambulance on the way. Does he have a shot in his bag called Glucagon? It's usually in a red plastic case. Diabetics carry them for times like these, when they go too low. It could revive him and keep him from going into a coma."

Coma. Revive. She fucking said revive!

My hands shook even harder and the man seemed to see that I was promptly about to lose my shit, so he took the phone from me and put it on speaker. Bending down, I checked the big part of his backpack. Other than the empty gun case and his insulin pen, nothing was in there.

Fuck.

"Ethan!" I screamed, completely losing my shit.

He wasn't moving.

With shaking hands, I peeled open the front of his backpack and there was a plastic red case.

Relief poured through me as I picked it up and

read the package. *Glucagon.* Prying it open, I grabbed the needle and inserted it into the jar of liquid that came with it. There was a powder and it needed to mix together.

The dude was relaying everything I did to the 911 lady.

"Stick him in the thigh with it, honey. Don't be afraid to hurt him. It needs to go in deep."

Holding the needle in the air, Ethan unconscious on the ground, something knocked me right in the gut and struck even more fear into my bones.

I was falling in love with him.

With a fearful cry, I shoved the shot into his leg and plunged the contents of the syringe into his bloodstream.

Two days ago, I'd taken blood from a classmate without so much as a rise in my heartbeat. Everything was different when it was someone you cared about.

"I did it!" I shouted, crawling down on to my elbows to stroke Ethan's forehead.

"Okay, honey, great job. The paramedics are on their way. You did really good."

A whimper lodged in my throat. He wasn't waking up. "Is he going to be okay?"

Silence.

"I'm sure he'll be fine, honey."

That wasn't an answer. That wasn't said with confidence. That was something you said to someone in panic so that they didn't spiral out.

Breathe. Just breathe.

I didn't realize my fingers were on his pulse, making sure his heart was still beating, until the EMTs showed up and pried them off.

"Are you family?" they asked me.

Ethan and Angela were literally the only people in the world who cared about me. Who would realize if I went missing or care if I died? If that wasn't fucking family, I didn't know what was.

"Yes," I croaked.

Ethan and I might not have shared even a kiss yet, but somehow he'd taken me in like a stray puppy and we were family. I knew in that moment that if things never got intimate between us and we decided to keep things platonic, that we would always be friends. He would always pick up when I called.

The next hour was a blur. I was in shock. I rode in the ambulance, and the men said that me giving him the glucagon shot might have saved his life. After we'd arrived at the hospital, the doctors grilled me on his insulin. How much did he take, how often, was it short acting or long? I didn't know anything and it made me feel so helpless. They'd hung an IV bag of straight glucose in the ambulance and Ethan had regained consciousness just as they were wheeling him into intensive care. Away from me.

Now I waited. I didn't know who to call. His brother was in jail, and he didn't talk to his parents. I could have texted Cody, but I wasn't sure if he'd want the guys knowing about this. So I just sat there in the same hospital I was born in and stared at the same piece of peeling pink wallpaper for nearly an hour, all the while going over scenarios in my head.

Why didn't I kiss him yet?

I was scared of him hurting me, that's why.

But now I was scared he could die without me ever getting the chance to kiss him. What would I say to him when he woke up? What if this happened again? My mind spun like a dryer on high until the doctor came out.

"Family of Ethan King."

I leapt up. "That's me! Is he okay?"

The doctor motioned for me to enter a more private room.

Answer the question, motherfucker! Is he okay? I wanted to scream but forced myself to stay civil.

He looked at his papers. "Okay, Ethan King, type one diabetic, was brought in—"

I grabbed the doctor's arm. "Is. He. Okay?"

He looked up from his papers and I could see the bags under his eyes more clearly. He was too young to be a seasoned veteran, probably a fucking intern.

"Yeah, he's fine. It looks like he took his long-acting insulin this morning instead of his short acting."

The breath I hadn't realized I'd been holding whooshed out of me. "Thank God."

The doctor went on: "The long acting insulin is only given once a day. He took it last night and this morning. Basically a double dose and it brought him too low. It could have been avoided had he been wearing a continuous glucose monitor. I'm surprised he doesn't have one."

Whatever it was, we needed it. "What is it and how can we get one?"

The doctor nodded. "It's a little device the size of a quarter that he wears on his abdomen. A small catheter reads the interstitial fluid, giving him a constant reading of the blood sugars, which he won't even feel. He changes it out every two weeks and it sends the continuous glucose readings to his phone. It will sound the alarm if he's too high, too low, or falling too fast."

Jesus, why didn't he have one? "Can you get us one?"

He nodded again, like a robot. "I'll write a prescription. Hopefully his insurance covers it. They can be pricey."

They better fucking cover it. I didn't have the tits to be a stripper.

He scribbled a few more things down on his paper. "You're his … fiancée? You live together?"

I may or may not have thrown the F word around when hospital admitting came by. "Yes. We live together."

Not a total lie.

"You can set your smartphone to get alerts as well. So if he drops too low during sleep, it will set off an alarm and you can wake him."

Guess who was finally getting a smart phone. Ethan was worth it. I didn't care how much it cost.

"Thank you so much. Can I … see him now?"

The doctor did another little bobblehead nod. "Yeah, we just want to monitor him another few hours and then he can go home."

"That's it? He almost dies and we'll be home in a few hours?" They must need the empty bed.

The doctor shrugged. "Unfortunately, this is common in diabetics. They get too low or too high and need to come in to be medically managed. Then we send them out again. He looks like he's in shape and eats well. I'm sure we won't be seeing you again anytime soon."

You bet your fucking life you wouldn't.

"Thank you. Please don't forget that prescription."

I was about to make sure Ethan King never stepped foot in this place again.

TEN

I stood outside room 137 with sweaty palms and a dry tongue. A whirlwind of emotions was rocking through me and I didn't know what I was going to say to him, or do to him.

Mount him? Slap him? I was almost mad at myself that I'd let myself fall for someone again. Caring for someone was nice, until it brought you pain.

"I can see your feet," Ethan's raspy voice came from inside.

Fuck.

I opened the door, plastered a fake smile on, and entered the room.

"Hey. How are you?" He looked pale, an IV in his arm and hospital sheet across his lap.

He held my gaze with his cobalt blue eyes and tracked me as I crossed the room to stand by his side. When I was close enough to touch him, I instinctively reached out and held his hand.

"I'm fine. But how are you?" There was concern laced in every word. This was *so* Ethan. He almost died and he was concerned with how I am.

"That was scary," I admitted, chewing my lip.

He reached up, tilting my chin so that I would meet his gaze. "I'm sorry I scared you."

The tears came then; the shock had worn off and now it was time for the emotional release. A sob formed in my throat and he opened his arms so that I could fall into them. Careful not to sit on his IV, I sat on the bed and let him hold me.

"I'm supposed to be the one comforting you!" I laughed into his chest as I wiped my tears.

He chuckled. "Nah, I like it better this way."

Sitting up, I brushed the tears off my cheeks again.

"Starting tomorrow, I'm making you a med chart. You put an X next to short acting or long acting. Okay?"

He grinned. "Yes, Nurse Hailey."

I sighed, staring at his chest. "I ... thought you were going to die."

His arms wrapped tighter around me. "I'm not going anywhere."

That simple statement put me at ease and I didn't know how badly I needed to hear it.

WHILE ETHAN SHOWERED ALL the hospital gunk off, I ran to the pharmacy and the AT&T store. An hour later, I walked in with the bag holding Ethan's new four-hundred-dollar device and my new six-hundred-dollar iPhone. Yep. I'd just put a grand on my credit card.

Fuck it. I didn't know Ethan's financial situation, but I knew he had to work hard to keep up the life-style he lived. I didn't want him to have to worry about money at a time like this.

When I walked in to the kitchen and saw Ethan sitting at the table, hair still wet from a shower, my inner nurse kicked in. He waited patiently, watching me, as I read over the instructions and pulled out the sensor that needed to be imbedded under his skin.

"Lift up your shirt," I commanded.

A sly grin crossed his face and I blushed.

I held the device up and clarified my intent. "So I can put this thing on."

He lifted his shirt over his head and took it off completely, dropping it on the table. And all the oxygen got sucked from the room.

Ethan King was a sculpture. His body was a work of art and I was so close to touching it. Reaching out, I lay my fingers on his stomach, feeling the taut muscles there.

Jesus, I could buy a dozen vibrators and it wouldn't replace this.

Rock. Hard. Ethan.

"This might hurt a bit." My voice cracked.

"Pain doesn't bother me." His voice was deep and husky, and for some reason his comment about pain was hot as fuck to me right now.

I swallowed hard, trying to remember what the directions had said and trying not to think about what it would be like to kiss him.

I'll bet he was a good kisser. *I bet he looks stellar naked too.*

After taking a cleansing breath, I disinfected the area, holding the device up to his skin. I pushed button that would embed the tiny needle-like catheter, and it shot into him with a snapping sound. I flinched. He didn't.

After clicking in the transmitter, I stepped back and surveyed my work.

"That's it?" He looked down at the small device the size of a quarter.

I nodded, picking up my phone and opening the app that came with it.

"It's syncing."

His eyes landed on the smart phone in my hand. "Did you get that just now? For me?"

My heart hammered in my chest as I realized just how deeply into him I was.

I nodded, not meeting his eyes. "I told you, you scared me. This way I can make sure you're safe."

His blood sugar level then popped up on the screen.

107.

Stable.

I sighed in relief, feeling all of my tight muscles relax. "Okay. You're good right now, but I should start dinner. Have you had your short acting insulin today? Where are the hospital's discharge instructions? I forgot what they—"

Ethan stood, and took my hand into his, setting my phone down on the table and stopping me mid-sentence.

"Hailey, I'm so sorry I scared you." His gaze was so sincere that it cut right into my broken soul.

He'd almost died. He'd been taken to the hospital

in an ambulance, and his one regret was that he'd scared *me*.

Ethan King was too pure for this shitty world. I didn't deserve him; I'd break him no doubt.

He was staring at me, intensely, inches from my face, unmoving.

Kiss him.

Part of me wanted to pop up on my tiptoes and suck his bottom lip into my mouth. But my other half was scared. Scared of what it would mean for Ethan and I, scared of having a panic attack or being a horrible kisser, scared of everything. So much fear. Fear had me trapped.

He reached out slowly, giving me a chance to pull away if I wanted, and stroked my neck, causing my legs to nearly buckle.

Leaning in, he pressed his lips right up to my ear: "When's the last time someone made love to you? Put your needs before theirs, didn't rest until every *inch* of you was pleasured."

Holy Fuck.

Ethan had a brush with death and now he was going for it. Big time.

And I wanted him to.

I gulped. Bryce was the only guy I'd been with, and pleasuring me wasn't high on his list.

"Never," I panted.

Stop.

Don't stop.

Anxiety and desire warred within me as Ethan brushed his lips to my neck and trailed it down my collarbone.

What if I scared him off? What if I broke him? What if we fell in love? What if he broke me? My mind was working overdrive, but my body, my body wasn't scared one bit. Not. At. All. It was green lights flashing as far as that was concerned. Heat pooled in my belly and a low throbbing started between my legs.

After brushing his lips across my collarbone, he pulled away and held his face right in front of mine, unmoving, with a piercing gaze.

I realized then that he wouldn't make the first move. He would wait, like a loyal dog, until I gave the command. Because he respected me; he cared. And that ignited something within me.

Fuck it. I was going for it.

"Kiss me," I commanded before I lost my nerve.

A slow smirk crossed his face then. His hand came up to gently cup the back of my neck. Stepping closer to me, he pressed his body flush against mine and I swear to God I moaned. He hadn't even done anything yet and I fucking moaned like I was having an orgasm. This was so long overdue; I'd fantasized about this moment for so long.

Leaning forward, he captured my mouth, pressing his lips to mine, and I immediately parted them, letting his tongue brush with mine. For a man as strong and big as Ethan King, his kiss was tender, delicate, fucking hot as hell. I was in control; he was letting me lead.

I pushed my pelvis into his, feeling pride at the hardness I felt there. I did that to him, I turned him on. He deepened the kiss as my arms went around his back, stroking the tight, corded muscles there, relishing the exposed part of my skin that touched his. His warm slick tongue entwined with mine and the kiss became more insistent. When his hands trailed down my back to cup my ass, I spread my legs so he could pull me up on him.

It's like Ethan was psychic. Everything I wanted him to do, he did. When my ankles hooked behind his back and I was fully straddling his waist, I decided to take it one step further. Letting him hold me up, I pulled away from our kiss to pull my shirt over my head, exposing my black lace bra.

Target clearance aisle score.

His eyes were blazing, chest heaving, lips

blushing red. He took one look at my bra and leaned forward, still holding me up, and placed his mouth around my nipple. The moment his tongue came out and sucked my lacy nipple into his mouth, pleasure exploded inside of me. I ground my hips into his hardness, wanting more.

What I felt between my legs, even through his basketball shorts, was big. Really big. And that scared me and excited me at the same time. In an expert move, he used one hand to unclasp my bra while walking me back to his bedroom. The moment my breasts were free, I threaded my fingers through his hair and pushed his face into them. And he obliged. Wrapping his mouth around my now bare nipple, he lapped at it with his tongue, nearly sending me over the edge.

Holy fuck, this was better than I ever dreamed, and we'd barely done anything.

Ethan lowered me onto the bed, leaning forward and taking my bottom lip into his mouth. His hands were on my breasts, thumbs lightly grazing my nipples, and I swore I was going to orgasm from this alone.

Oh how sexually deprived I had been? Ethan's nipple delight was going to make me go all the way.

When he pulled back and looked at me, his eyes were half lidded.

"Show me what you want," he breathed, and my mind went blank.

What did I want? I'd never been asked that in bed. Bryce was a "wham, bam, thank you, ma'am" kind of guy. I never really wanted anything from him. Even in our heyday, sex was a chore to please him.

"Surprise me," I finally said.

I trusted Ethan.

He grinned, and holy hell that smile alone made me wet.

Reaching down, he unbuttoned my jeans and peeled them off of me, kissing my thighs as he went. I didn't even give him time to pull off my undies, I yanked them off for him, spreading my legs wide. I was absolutely aching for his touch; I'd never wanted anything more in my life. Two firm hands planted themselves on either side of my thighs and then his face went southward and I lost all rational thought. It was just spurts of words and thoughts and feelings.

Licking.

Moaning.

Heat.

Throbbing.

I wanted to fucking explode.

My back arched, nails gritting into the pillow, as Ethan lapped my most sensitive spot. I thought, *This was it, this can't feel any better*, until he released one of his hands and inserted a finger inside of me.

"Ethan!" I shouted in pure bliss. His other hand came up to tweak my nipple as his tongue lapped harder, and the queen of all orgasms rocked my body. I think I blacked out, or went to another planet or something crazy. Time definitely stopped. Ethan King had magical time-stopping powers and all I was aware of was this wave of pleasure I'd been thrown into and my body never wanted to get off of. I ground my pelvis into him and rocked back and forth as the orgasm took me to other dimensions.

I'm throwing out my vibrator.

It's broken.

Nothing will ever feel good again unless it was from his mouth.

When I finally finished, I pulled his head up to look at him.

The bastard was wearing a cocky, lopsided grin.

"I've wanted to do that since that first night at Mickey's," he declared.

Now it was my time to grin. "I forgot how to speak."

The deep throaty chuckle that came from him left butterflies in my stomach. Leaning forward, he kissed the spot right between my breasts before pulling away. "Wash up. I'll make dinner."

I frowned. "What about you?"

I pointed to the giant erection tent that had popped up in his pants.

He winked. "Next time."

Ethan was a giver, and for our first time together I'd have to say I wasn't complaining. As he walked out of the room to make dinner, I found myself grinning.

I'd kissed another man and it felt good, it felt normal. I felt normal. That was the greatest gift Ethan could have ever given me. Second to that orgasm, which would go down in history.

ETHAN AND I WERE ... dating. *I think.* I mean, we hadn't talked about it, but we were definitely make-out buddies with some nightly foreplay thrown in there for good measure. It had been two weeks since my queen of all orgasms, and come to find out ... they were all like that. With Ethan they were.

We hadn't gone all the way yet; he wanted to

wait until I was sure. I assured him I was five hundred-percent sure, but still he stopped before the act every time. I wasn't complaining. We'd gotten really good at foreplay. Pleasuring each other without going all the way totally reminded me of high school.

My classes were going good, I was happy, and life was starting to feel normal for the first time in … ever. Bryce hadn't come around after the alleyway attack, and Ethan had put up security cameras in front of the shop. The hot summer was gone, bringing the cool Arizona winter; and Ethan's blood sugars were stable. Life was good.

I walked out from his bedroom, where I now slept most nights, unless I needed to be up late studying. He was poring over his laptop at the kitchen table.

His voice was full of excitement: "What are you doing this weekend?"

I opened the fridge and popped a grape in my mouth. "You?"

His eyes blazed and went half lidded as he took in my bare legs. "Cute. Snowbowl is opening. The boys and I are renting a cabin. Want to go skiing? You can bring Angela…"

Skiing. That simple word brought memories

with Bryce with it. We went to Aspen every year with his parents to ski, and I loved being on the mountain.

"I have two shifts. I'll see if I can get them covered," I told him.

He nodded. Reaching out, he grabbed the hem of my big t-shirt—actually it was his shirt—and yanked me closer to him.

Plopping on his lap, I slung an arm around his neck. I wasn't wearing a bra under this shirt but I had taken time to stop and put on undies. Not that it would matter. Ethan had a way of always taking those off, even when I thought we had no time. His hand slipped under my shirt and he ran a finger over my nipple.

"I'm booking us the master bedroom." His voice vibrated on my neck as his fingers brushed my nipples back and forth.

Hailey 2.0 was a sexual creature who could not get enough of Ethan King. Hooked up last night; will hook up again this morning; zero fucks given if that made me a nymphomaniac. There was no stopping point with Ethan. Every time felt new. And I wanted him all the time.

His hand slipped into my underwear and my eyes rolled into my head.

Screw breakfast.

When his fingers slid inside of me, I panted into his ear.

"I'm ready," I told him.

Fuck me, for God's sake! I wanted to scream.

He trailed his tongue along my neck, kissing my jawline as I threw my head back, grinding my pelvis into his hand.

Magic hands.

Magic fingers.

Magic tongue.

Everything about him was magic.

"This weekend, at the cabin," he huffed, stroking his thumb along my most delicate part. My nipples tightened, back arched, and holy hell I was having an orgasm at the breakfast table.

My brain worked enough to compute that Ethan would have sex with me if I went skiing this weekend, so you bet your ass I was getting out of work. Whatever it took.

"STREP THROAT?" Mickey said over the phone, and I felt bad for lying. I never lied to him, and I always wanted extra shifts, so this was really hard to pull off.

"Yeah," I croaked in an extra fake, scratchy voice, and prayed he didn't want a doctor's note.

"Alright, hun, no worries I'll have one of the other girls cover it."

"Okay, thanks, Mickey. I should be better in a few days."

"Rest up, baby girl. See you soon." He hung up and I grinned.

I'd gotten Angela to come as well. She wasn't scheduled at Mickey's but she'd had to beg, borrow, and steal to get someone to watch her kid for the weekend. She and Cody were hooking up, keeping things casual but definitely a thing. Nick was currently dating some mouthy Italian chick who was coming as well, while James and Sebastian were flying solo and sharing a room. Which we teased them about endlessly.

I packed light, hoping to buy a set of snow coveralls at the Wal-Mart in town. There was nothing in Phoenix. I wished I had my Salomons, but of course Bryce had those with him. Bryce had been joylessly silent over the past month, and I prayed that Ethan's beat-down had scared the shit out of him and run him out of town.

Ethan locked up the shop and we all rode together in a group, the girls hanging on to the boys while the five motorcycles weaved in and out of traffic. There was something powerful about riding in a group of motorcycles. I was happy to report that Ethan had bought a helmet and now wore it religiously.

When we stopped for gas, people gave us wary glances, especially since Ethan and the other boys were packing. Who in Arizona didn't have a gun at this point? I'd just gotten used to it, but the mothers clung a little tighter to their children when Ethan went in to pay for gas. Tatted-up felon, with his Kings Club leather vest on, I didn't blame them. But he was harmless—unless you pissed him off.

By the time we checked into the cabin Friday night, it was past 10PM and we all wanted to be up early for tackling the mountain. Ethan led me upstairs and the hallway split. To the right went Angela and Cody, and to the left was our master. Everyone else was downstairs. The windows and high ceilings made this place so dreamy. Light snow was falling outside, signaling the start of winter even though it was only the first week of November. It was an early ski season, and I was super stoked. As Ethan opened the double doors to the large master, I nearly gasped at the luxury. This reminded me of my old life for a second, but this time it was special; it was with Ethan. And after living life as a waitress, barely scraping by, it was everything to me in this moment.

A huge king bed lay in front of a roaring fire, already set up by the housekeeper. Double doors led out to a deck, where a hot tub sat waiting to be used. The master had a huge soaker tub and double-head shower. Granite counters, rich ebony cabinets—it was fabulous.

"You like it?" Ethan set his duffle bag down at the end of the bed and faced me.

I grinned. "I love it."

He looked pleased he could spoil me with this type of luxury. I'd never tell him that I lived this level of wealth every day for seven years; it would cheapen this moment and this was special to me. More special than when Bryce used his parents' money to buy me things.

He sat on the bed and started to unlace his riding boots, rolling his head back and forth to stretch his neck.

"Want a backrub?" I asked, laying my phone on the bed and kicking off my shoes.

He looked up at me with stormy eyes. "That's

not even a question. I'll never deny a backrub from you."

Laughter bubbled out of me as I grabbed the lotion bottle. I was pretty damn good at backrubs.

He grabbed his water bottle and chugged. "I have a headache. Long drive."

After peeling off his shirt, he lay face forward on the bed.

Headache? Was that code for he didn't want to have sex tonight as promised? Or did he really have a headache?

I shrugged it off and started to massage him, straddling his back. When he moaned, every arousal point in my body lit up.

"Damn, woman," he growled as I dug in deep near his shoulder, "you're so good at this."

That caused a smile to pull at my lips. I was straddling his back, and as I leaned forward to kiss his neck my phone buzzed. Not a normal buzz, this was a continuous rhythm, the alert buzz from his glucose device I'd paired with my phone.

I launched off of him like my ass was on fire and fumbled for my phone. "How are you feeling?" I asked nervously, ready to call 911. His phone was going off too.

He sat up and sighed as we both looked at my screen.

310.

WAY too fucking high.

"Fuck. I'll bet that fast food place didn't give me diet soda like I asked for. It tasted too sweet, but I ignored it."

Those motherfuckers! I was going to call and rip them a new asshole tomorrow. How dare they screw up his order and nearly kill him.

"Ethan! What do we do?" My heart was jack-knifing in my chest and my fingers were ready to speed-dial 911. Some nurse I was going to be. All my hair would fall out by my second patient.

Leaning forward, he placed a kiss on my nose. "I'm going to take my fast acting insulin and in thirty minutes I'll be fine. Don't worry so much." Then he stood and moved across the room to head for the kitchen like it was no big deal. Like a blood sugar of 310 was no fucking big deal.

The second he left the room, my fingers went tapping on Google. 310 *blood sugar. Dangers of high blood sugar. How long does it take for short acting insulin to work? When to go to the hospital for high blood sugar.*

By the time he got back to the room, I'd totally freaked myself out.

"Maybe we should go to the hospital to be safe."

He chuckled. "Hailey, if I went to the hospital every time I had high blood sugar, I would live there. Check it now. I'll bet it's already going down."

I glanced at the app. 270.

Relief exploded in my chest. Okay, no worries. He was going to be fine.

He sat down next to me and slung an arm around my shoulder. "Did you Google while I was gone?"

I gave him a guilty look and he just laughed. "Don't they teach you about Dr. Google in nursing school?"

Yeah, they actually did. "It's different when it's someone you care about."

His face softened. Reaching out, he tucked a stray chunk of hair behind my ear. "I care about you too. That's why I don't want you worrying about me."

Easier said than done. He looked so tired. Tonight wasn't the best night for our first time. "Wanna go to bed?"

He sighed, rubbing his eyes. "I'm beat."

"You get some sleep." I ran my fingers through his dark hair. "I'm just going to stay up a bit longer."

And watch these numbers like a hawk until they were under two hundred.

He smirked. "Sorry I ruined the mood. Tomorrow night, you, me, and that hot tub." He pointed outside to the balcony.

I grinned, leaning forward and captured his mouth in a kiss. Pulling away, I met his gaze. "Tomorrow night."

Desire flashed across his face and I knew without a doubt that twenty-four hours from now I'd be having the hottest sex of my life.

ELEVEN

W e'd just got to the bottom of the ski hill and I had a light dusting of powdered snow on my jacket. Angela and I'd gone to Wal-Mart on the way into town and had gotten snow pants, jacket, gloves, and goggles for under a hundred bucks.

Cody cut his snowboard to the side and pulled off his goggles. "Damn, Hailey, where did you learn to shred like that? You're awesome."

Ethan pulled in behind him. I'd been the one to get to the bottom of the hill first. Where did I learn to shred? *Private lessons in Aspen.*

I dodged the question. "Thanks, man, I love skiing."

Angela came down the hill next, screaming for dear life.

"I'm going to die!" she shrilled.

"Make a pizza with your skis!" I reminded her. It was our fourth run down and Angela had let slip on the drive up to the mountain that she'd never skied before. Now I was giving her little lessons, but she was still scared of stopping.

She did as I asked and made the pizza with her skis, but still somehow managed to crash into the back of Ethan's snowboard and take him down.

He growled at her before rolling onto his side.

"Sorry." She winced from flat on her back, sprawled in the snow.

Then he laughed and we all laughed, because people wiping out and falling was funny shit.

Sebastian, Ethan's shop manager, came down next, and right after him was Mr. Silent, the sexy firefighter James. I was pretty sure that Nick and his flavor of the month had run off to have sex somewhere.

"I'm famished," Cody called out.

My stomach grumbled. Skiing burned like a million calories. No matter how much food you ate, you were always hungry on the mountain.

"Yes."

Ethan unclipped his board after helping Angela up. "I could go for some hot chili right about now."

Mmmm, chili.

Our little crew made our way inside the lodge, ditching our ski stuff to sit in the racks and get snowed on.

After I got a cup of chili, a side of mac and cheese, french fries, *and* hot chocolate, we found a table.

No one spoke for a good ten minutes. We just inhaled calories and carbs like it was air. One thing I loved about Ethan was that he was healthy. Dating a diabetic who constantly pounded candy and pie would bug me to the end of the earth. He was responsible with his diet, going for low carb and high protein, rarely sugar. His nightly dessert back at home was a small cup of fresh berries with yogurt.

Today he'd gotten a cup of chili and a cheese-burger wrapped in lettuce, no bun. When he took a swig of his diet coke my brain went to a completely irrational place after his blood sugar going too high last night. *Was* it diet coke? I mean, the machine was labeled Diet Coke and I'd seen him dispense it ... *But what if one of these teenage stoners back there put the wrong soda in there?*

Man, was I always this neurotic?

"Can I have a sip?" I asked on the sly. I could

determine if it were diet or not, because that shit tasted nasty.

Ethan grinned, giving me a knowing look. "Relax. It's diet."

Busted. I feigned ignorance. "I know. I just want a sip, my hot chocolate tastes weird," I lied.

Again with his grin and knowing look.

The others were locked in a rabid discussion about our current president when Ethan handed me the drink and leaned over to whisper in my ear. "You're cute when you're being Nurse Hailey." His lips caressed my ear at the same time his hand squeezed my thigh.

Four ski runs was enough, right? We should probably go back to our hotel room now.

When he pulled back, I gave him "the look," the look a woman gives a man when they want sex. There's nothing subtle about it; I might or might not have even bit my lip, causing him to grin wider. Ethan smiling was the best damn thing in the world. Some guys get uglier when they smiled—sorry, but it's true. Some just stay the same. But Ethan, ohhh, Ethan, got ten degrees hotter when he grinned.

I was just about to retort with something sexy when I saw Bryce walk into the lodge with his parents and search the space with his eyes like he was looking for someone.

My stomach turned to stone as my mouth hung slack.

That motherfucker. Fear and anger washed over me, which was an improvement from straight-up fear. I was getting stronger.

Ethan saw the change in my face and turned to follow my gaze.

"Oh hell no." He stood. "Boys ... that's Bryce."

It was like he'd pointed out the devil incarnate to them. Sebastian, Cody, and James simultaneously dropped their food and stood, chests puffed out, ready to attack. The mere mention of Bryce's name was enough to invoke their rage.

Bryce's parents spent the snow season in Aspen. EVERY season. Why the hell were they here? The moment Bryce's gaze landed on mine, he gave a lopsided grin.

I looked at Ethan to see the veins were popped out of his neck, fists clenched. A steely glare settled in his gaze, aimed right at my psycho ex. The last time they'd seen each other was in the ally at Mickey's. Ethan had threatened to kill him if he ever touched me again.

Ethan looked down at me and his face softened.

"They are coming over here. Quickly, tell me two things. One, are his parents good people? I mean, do you want to keep them in your life?"

My answer was instant. "No." His dad was an emotionally absent asshole who never showed love to anyone in the family. His mom was a victim somewhat, but I'd never forget when I told her Bryce had hit me. She'd been the only one I could talk to. She'd frowned and said. "Well, what did you do?"

They were both rotten apples.

"Second question, Hailey..." He bent down and met my gaze. "Do you think Bryce followed you here? Or is he just skiing with his family by accident?"

Ethan was trying to assess the level of stalker Bryce had become and so was I. I wanted to believe he was just on a vacation with his Beverly Hills parents in Podunk Flagstaff, at the never-heard-of Snowbowl Ski Mountain, but no ... they owned a three-million-dollar cabin in Aspen, and you couldn't pry his mother away from there once the snow came.

"He followed me," I breathed.

That was all Ethan needed. He stood, his back to me, and I looked up just in time to see Bryce and his parents walk up to us.

"Hailey!" Kitty Conner cooed, opening her arms

out to me. She was decked out in a Gucci snowsuit with fur lining, cheeks flushed from being out in the cold. Kitty didn't ski; she hung out at the Aspen lodge with her girlfriends and drank two bottles of wine. Ethan stepped in front of me, and Sebastian, Cody, and James flanked him. They had made a wall between me and my worst nightmare.

"Hailey doesn't have anything more to say to your family. I think you should leave." Ethan's voice was firm but slightly unhinged. I looked up between Sebastian's and James' shoulders to see Bryce looking right at me.

"Excuse me?" Kitty brought out her claws, hand on chest as she looked all kinds of offended. "What jail did you just escape from? I can talk to my daughter-in-law anytime I please."

Ethan took a deep breath. "She's not your family anymore. Walk. Away. Now."

The look on Kitty's face would forever go down in my memory as the greatest thing I'd ever seen. She looked like she was taking a shit. She was so mortally offended she'd been slapped into submission with nothing to say.

"Bryce, who is this?" his father asked, looking dumbfounded himself. He probably didn't even know we were divorced. He spent most of his time in Europe with his mistress.

"Her new fuck toy," Bryce said coolly, keeping his gaze on me.

"Bryce!" Kitty smacked his shoulder, but his eyes were pinned on me and wouldn't leave. Ethan stepped forward, coming right up in Bryce's face and opening the wall so that his parents could finally see me. I hope they saw the terror. The scars I wore were invisible.

"Stop looking at her or I'll rip your eyes out of your head and shove them up your ass," Ethan growled.

His parents collectively gasped, but Bryce just grinned, like he was enjoying getting under Ethan's skin. He was poking the bear on purpose. He'd planned this. His gaze was still on me and I held it, pushing every ounce of hatred I could into my face. Ethan's hand came up lightning-quick and grabbed Bryce's jaw, forcing him to look away from me.

"Touch me and go to jail!" Bryce spat, ripping his face away from Ethan.

James, Sebastian, and Cody both laughed, making Bryce look at the men warily.

Now Ethan was grinning, sinister and powerful. "Send me to jail, motherfucker. I'll spend some quality time with my big brother there. Meanwhile, when you go to jail, I'll make sure they give you a nice welcome party." Ethan winked.

Kitty gasped and grabbed her son's arm: "This is why I didn't want to come here! Trash. All of them." She yanked Bryce away, but I saw it, the deadly look my ex had given Ethan for embarrassing him in front of his parents; it gave me chills. Ethan was a badass, and I had no doubt that he was capable of murder if it meant protecting me, but Bryce ... I was starting to think Bryce was an unhinged psychopath and Ethan would push him over the edge.

Ethan turned to me then, placing two gentle hands on either side of my arms. "Are you okay?"

I hadn't even needed to say one word to Bryce or his family. Ethan had protected me from all of that. Still, seeing them here had shaken me. Watching them leave out the double doors should have made me feel better, but I was worried.

I nodded. "But you need to be careful. Bryce is dangerous," I warned him.

James, who rarely spoke, stepped closer to Ethan and lowered his voice. "Say the word and I'll help you kill him and hide the body." His voice was low and deadly and his words sent chills up my spine. He wasn't kidding.

I should be scared. They were talking about murder. Any normal person would have immediately jumped in with "No! Don't even say that!" But I didn't. I stayed silent. Some deep dark part of me wanted Bryce dead. Then maybe I could sleep peacefully at night. He'd gone too far dragging his parents here. He was sick in the head, I could see that now. He wasn't going to let me go.

Ethan placed a hand on James' shoulder. "Thanks, brother, but that won't be necessary." He paused before looking at me. "Yet."

There was a promise in his eyes. My sexy felon would wipe the Earth of Bryce Conner if he fucked with me again.

"Do you want to go back to the cabin?" Angela asked, speaking up for the first time, timid and shy for once in her life.

I sighed. "No. Then he wins. I want to ski all day with my friends like planned." I tipped my chin high and stared at the double doors Kitty had dragged Bryce through. She wouldn't stay on the mountain after that skirmish. They were probably on their way back to Phoenix now, soon to be on a plane to Aspen.

The others dispersed while Ethan pulled me into his chest. I tucked my head underneath his chin and just let him hold me, right there in the middle of the crowded lodge. Pulling back, he tilted my chin up so that he could look into my eyes.

"Let's have fun while we are here, but when we get back to Phoenix I think we should meet with a lawyer or police officer and talk about your options."

My options. Like a restraining order? I couldn't get one of those without iron-clad proof that Bryce was stalking or abusing me. So far I had a paid-off credit card and a random meet-up at a ski resort. Nothing that would hold up in court. What he'd done in the alley behind Mickey's wasn't on tape, and I'd never reported it for fear of Ethan going to jail for assault. But I didn't want Ethan to worry, so I nodded.

I was determined to enjoy my weekend, Bryce wouldn't ruin tonight for me. Ethan, the hot tub. I deserved that, and I wouldn't let Bryce wreck this new relationship that I'd built. It might have been built over a burning fire, but I'd built it nonetheless, and I was finally happy and feeling normal. That's all I'd wanted since I left L.A. Ethan King was my ticket out of victim hell and I wasn't going to lose that. I cared for him too much.

Bryce could go fuck himself. I could deal with a few random meet-ups here and there. But if he ever touched me again, Ethan or I would put a bullet in his head.

———

I TRIED NOT to let Bryce's little run-in ruin my day, but I'd be lying if I said I wasn't looking over my shoulder the rest of the time we spent skiing. By 3PM we were all wiped out and made our way back to the SUV we'd rented for the day to get us up and down the snowy mountain. When Ethan opened the back SUV gate and found Nick and his girl half naked doing God knows what, we all burst out laughing. Ethan kicked them out of the car and chastised them for being teenagers, but it lightened the mood.

By the time 5PM rolled around, we were grilling burgers on the deck in a snowy wonderland and I'd all but forgotten Bryce's run-in. I'd napped a little when we got home, and now I was excited to eat, jump into the hot tub with Ethan, and then have our special night together.

He came out onto the porch holding his riding helmet.

I raised an eyebrow. "Going somewhere?"

He leaned in and kissed my cheek. "Getting a few things to make tonight special," he whispered.

"Be back for dinner in thirty minutes, and then hot tub."

Heat traveled down my body at his promise, and my heart beat wildly at the romantic gesture. Was he getting flowers? Chocolate with strawberries? Champagne?

I watched him walk out the door. Then Angela came over to hip bump me. "Wanna play Cards of Humanity with James, Cody and I until dinner is ready?"

"Sure." I followed her inside and we started to play while Sebastian tended the grill. I sort of lost track of time until Sebastian declared burgers were ready.

Ethan wasn't back.

I picked up my phone and texted him.

Burgers are ready.

No reply.

Sitting down, I slowly picked at my meal and decided to check his blood sugar through my app. What if he went really low while he was driving and got in an accident, or was lying unconscious on a grocery store floor?

120.

Normal.

Minutes ticked on and I barely could focus on what the guys were saying.

Excited for tonight but I don't need fancy stuff. Come home. I texted.

No reply. It was late now, an hour had gone by, and I was seriously worried. I couldn't just sit here.

I stood. "I'm gonna go look for Ethan. I'm worried."

Nick looked up at me. "Relax, mama, he's probably trying to decide which condoms to buy."

His date barked out in laughter, but no one else did.

James, my silent hero, stood. "I'll drive you. We can check out the local grocery store."

It was a small town, there weren't many places he could be, and it had been almost an hour now. Roads were slushy with ice and I was officially panicking.

Pulling out my phone again, I called him and got the busy signal.

What the fuck? My stomach sank.

"I feel like something terrible has happened," I told James, on the verge of tears as he grabbed the SUV keys.

"Let's have a look around. Hopefully we'll laugh

about this when he shows up saying he got stuck in the snow or something."

Maybe his bike did get stuck in the snow, although there wasn't much snow down here; it was all up on the mountain. And why wasn't his phone working?

I focused on my breathing, trying in vain to text and call Ethan like a psycho girlfriend.

James pulled out of the neighborhood where we were renting the cabin and we drove in silence for a few minutes. No music, no talking, just the frantic beating of my heart.

As we pulled out onto Milton Road, the road that took you to the grocery store, my heart leapt into my throat.

There was an ambulance. The sun was setting, and just seeing the flashing lights had my stomach in knots.

"Fuck! That's Ethan's bike," James muttered, just as the ambulance took off, sirens blaring.

Oh fuck. Oh no. Oh God.

My hands shook as I tried to remember to breathe. James gunned it and tailed the ambulance, but as we passed Ethan's crumpled bike, my eyes went wide and tears streamed down my face, blurring my vision. I spun around frantically looking for a car or anyone that could have hit him, but it was just his bike, lying there in the median, a bag of strawberries and broken bottle of champagne spilled out into the street. A sob formed in my throat. There wasn't much snow on the ground in town; I didn't see any ice.

Maybe he hit an ice patch that I couldn't see. *Oh God*. Why did he go to the store? I didn't need special shit.

Please don't die, I prayed. My heart couldn't take it. James reached across the car and took my hand into his, squeezing it tightly.

"He was wearing his helmet. He will be okay," James said in an almost robotic voice.

I was glad James was with me, because I couldn't think straight, I couldn't talk right. I was in shock.

After getting to the hospital, James questioned the front desk lady within an inch of her life. He would have made a good police interrogator, all scary and demanding. I just stood there and mumbled that he was diabetic three or four times, not knowing what else to say.

Ethan had only been brought in a few moments ago. They were still assessing his injuries, but he'd been wearing his helmet, so that was looking good. I focused on the helmet and thanked God a million times that I'd made him start wearing one.

What if he couldn't walk? What if he needed a lung transplant because a broken rib punctured his? My inner Nurse Hailey went to all the dark places.

"Can you tell us anything?" James barked at the front desk lady for the twentieth time.

She glared at James. "I can tell you that we are doing everything we can to help your friend and I'll send a doctor or nurse out to speak to you shortly."

Then she slammed her glass door shut, cutting us off.

"I gotta call the boys." James looked a bit unhinged. "We lost a buddy to a motorcycle accident a few years ago. He was a new member of the crew. It was … bad. Accidents are bad."

Maybe I wasn't the only one losing my shit. "I'll call them," I told him, and he gave me a grateful smile.

While James sat, rubbing his hands through his hair, I called Angela and told her the news.

"Holy fuck, girl!" she screamed. She said they were on their way. Everyone showed up, including douchebag Nick and his girl.

We overflowed that waiting room. Four danger-ous-looking biker dudes and three chicks who didn't know what to do with themselves. It felt like hours before a nurse finally walked through the double doors. She was wearing a surgical cap and had blood on her scrubs.

Ethan's blood?

"Family of Ethan King?" she called.

We all stood.

When she raised an eyebrow, I stepped forward. "I'm a nurse. What's going on?"

Okay, slight lie, I was a nursing student, but she wasn't going to check my credentials, and it might get me back there.

She nodded, stepping forward. "Mr. King was in an accident and sustained multiple injuries. We're taking him back to surgery, but he's stable. I just wanted you to know."

Accident. Multiple injuries. Surgery.

"What ... kind of injuries?" I pressed her.

What if he was brain damaged or couldn't work with his hands anymore? He loved working on motorcycles more than anything.

She gave me an apologetic smile. "Hard to tell until we get in there. Nothing seems internal. Shattered femur for sure, definitely broken ribs."

Angela burst into tears and I literally felt my soul leave my body. Shattered femur meant months in a cast and at least a year of physical therapy. But he was alive. And his organs were okay.

I nodded, trying to keep the tears inside. "Thank you."

She turned to leave and then spun back around. "Oh, and I've called the police. They'll come by after he's recovered to take his statement."

I frowned as James stood from his seat. "Statement?" the strong and silent biker asked.

She nodded. "Before we delivered anesthesia to him, Ethan told us that it was a hit and run. I'll be back as soon as I can."

She left out the double doors and my whole world came crashing down.

Hit and run.

Hit and run.

Hit and run.

Hit and run.

Those words spun around and around in my head until I felt sick.

Bryce wouldn't ... he wouldn't go that far, would he?

"Fucking four-wheeled bastards think they own the road!" Sebastian kicked a chair, causing others to look our way.

They started to gripe about how no one watches

out for motorcycles while I stewed in my nightmare of all nightmare juices.

Would Bryce try to kill Ethan?

No. That was too far, even for Bryce.

Hit and runs happened all the time. Probably a drunk driver.

Cody came over and slung an arm around me. "He'll be okay. He's the strongest guy I've ever met."

I just nodded. But in that moment I remembered the look Bryce had given Ethan at the ski lodge. It was ... deadly.

TWELVE

Twelve hours. Twelve fucking hours of waiting and not knowing what the hell was happening to the man who had repaired my injured heart. Sitting here in the hospital not knowing if he was seriously injured, it made me realize something.

Somewhere along the way I'd fallen in love with Ethan King.

This was bad news. Awful news. Everyone I loved got hurt, including me. Over the past twelve hours I had convinced myself that Bryce had forced Ethan off the road in an effort to kill him. I was sure of it, and I was going to tell the police they'd had an argument at the lodge. I owed that to Ethan. No more hiding and allowing Bryce to get away with shit.

When the nurse finally came back, looking bleary-eyed and tired, I shook everyone awake. They'd all fallen asleep. Only James and I had kept pounding the coffee and stayed awake to see this through. I would crash later. Ethan needed me.

"How is he?" I stepped forward, nearly tripping over my own feet.

She nodded. "Stable. Cat scan shows no brain injury thanks to the helmet. Two orthopedic surgeons had to work together to rebuild his leg. He's got enough metal pins and plates to set off airport security, but he'll be okay."

It hit me then, the relief, and I burst into tears.

"Thank you," I mumbled between sniffles.

She nodded. "He's waking up from anesthesia now, and the police officer is waiting to speak with him. After that, you can go in. Only one of you. He'll spend the night in the ICU because he's diabetic."

I nodded. "Actually, I'd like to speak with that officer. I have a tip for him." I held my head high and James, Sebastian, and Cody froze. Nick was still passed out.

"You don't think?" James whispered to me.

The nurse frowned. "I'll send him out."

Then she left.

I turned to face James. His blond hair was

smooshed on one side from leaning against the wall half the night.

"Bryce is capable of this. I see that now," I told him as my heart thumped in my chest.

James's jaw grit. "I'll fucking kill that punk if he did this. Are you sure?"

No, I wasn't sure of anything. "I'm going to tell the police they got in a scuffle at the lodge and have them go right now to check out the front of Bryce's car and his alibi."

James relaxed a little at that, but Sebastian stepped forward, fists clenched. "Maybe I should pay a little visit to Bryce before the cops do...?"

I shook my head. "No, we need to be sure, and this has to go on record if we want to put Bryce away."

He looked let down but nodded.

I started to pace the halls. Was Bryce in a rental? Or his white Range Rover? Had he gotten a new car since then? Were there streetlight cameras here? It was a small town. Would his parents lie to give him an alibi? My thoughts were swirling around in my head when the male police office stepped out of the double doors and called me into a private side room to take my statement.

Twenty minutes after my panicked ramble, he

looked at his notes. "So your boyfriend and your ex-husband got into an argument at the ski lodge and then your boyfriend later went to the store and you think your ex tried to run him off the road?"

Wow, that made me sound really white trash and paranoid but I nodded. "Yes. Bryce has been ... abusive to me in the past. That's why we divorced." My voice was small ... but there, I'd said it out loud. I survived an abusive marriage.

The cop frowned. "Do you have that on record anywhere? File a complaint? A restraining order?"

Fuck.

"No. I just wanted out."

The cop sighed. "Next time take pictures, call us out to the scene and file a formal complaint. I can't do anything with hearsay."

I nodded. "I will. Can you check Bryce's car? Ask for his alibi?"

He tipped his head. "I'll go over there and see what comes out naturally, but without a warrant I won't be able to see his car unless it's parked outside."

My eyes widened. Bryce's family were fancy lawyer people. They wouldn't just let him poke around without a warrant. "Then get a warrant."

The cop looked down his nose at me. "How?

What evidence do I show a judge that your ex had beef with Ethan? Snowbowl Lodge doesn't have cameras. This is all hearsay, and the judge will tell me you are trying to get back at your ex for not leaving you with any money."

I'd told him Bryce was from a wealthy family and had connections.

"But it's not that," I whimpered.

The cop placed a hand light on my shoulder and gave me a compassionate look. "I want to believe you. I do. But I need evidence, okay?"

Desperation settled into my bones. "Okay."

And that was that. I didn't have anything on camera, no pictures, just a hunch...

After the cop left the room, I sat there questioning my sanity. Was I taking it too far by thinking Bryce would do this? He was an abusive asshole yeah, but he wouldn't just try to kill Ethan and ruin his life. Going to jail and losing his job and car and all his fancy trips, that was the last thing he would ever do. He wouldn't risk that.

Maybe I'd gone too far with my paranoia?

Sebastian was in the doorway. "What did he say?"

I needed to calm this situation or it was going to get out of hand. "He's going to look into it. Now I'm not so sure Bryce would have done this. I think I'm being paranoid."

Sebastian gave me a look and was silent for a moment. "If we find out he did, he's dead," was all the biker said before going into the next room.

I sat there rubbing my hands together in an anxious gesture until the nurse came back.

"I can take you to see him now."

As I stood and followed her down the hall, I questioned whether I was really the best influence on Ethan's life.

HE WAS asleep when I walked in, lying on the bed hooked up to a thousand wires and tubes. My gut dropped to see him in this condition. I immediately looked at his oxygen and heart rate and breathed a sigh of relief when the numbers looked stable. Next I glanced at his left leg, in a huge cast with steel pins sticking out of it. My throat tightened as I forced myself not to cry. I cared about this guy so much, and seeing him like this ... it killed me.

I sat down and slipped my fingers into his warm, limp hand, and then leaned my head forward on the edge of the bed. The sterile disinfectant smell invaded my nostrils and I found my thoughts racing at a hundred miles an hour. Did Bryce do this? Should I have even jumped into a relationship so quickly after my divorce? I wasn't sure I could handle losing Ethan. I'd stupidly already become so attached. How could I nail Bryce's ass to the wall and get him in jail, where he could no longer taunt me or anyone I cared about? These thoughts spun around and around until the lack of sleep pulled me into the darkness.

A warm hand on my shoulder woke me and my eyes snapped open. I was no longer holding Ethan's hand, my face was lying on his hip. Jerking my head up, I saw him look down at me, his hand on my shoulder. He had a black eye and scratches on his cheek, and his gaze was hauntingly sad.

"We've got to stop having dates in the hospital," he declared.

I burst into tears, and then laughter, reaching out to grasp his good hand. "How's your pain?"

He nodded. "I'm high as fuck right now." Then he pointed to a morphine pump beside his bed.

I cracked a smile. His sense of humor and lack of pain brought me some form of relief. Reaching out, he grasped my face and gently ran his finger over my lips. "I'm sorry this happened, if I scared you."

I frowned. "Don't be. It's not your fault."

He shook his head. "The roads were slick. I shouldn't have taken my bike. I shouldn't have even gone to the store."

He was beating himself up. "No, hey, don't say that. You're a great driver."

He was. Always safe. And played by the rules.

I wanted to scream that I thought Bryce did this. It was burning a hole in my tongue, but I didn't want to upset him.

He sighed and looked up at the ceiling. "I'm glad to be alive." Then he looked at me. "To be with you."

My heart fluttered. "I'm glad to be with you too." I leaned closer, careful not to hurt him, and ran my fingers through his hair.

"Hailey?" he whispered, his cobalt eyes looking right through me.

My heart beat wildly in my chest. "What?" I leaned even closer. What was he going to tell me? *Did he think it was Bryce too?*

"I probably shouldn't say this, because I'm totally high and not thinking right, but ... I'm so fucking in love with you. I didn't want to die without telling you that. Thank you for dropping your walls and letting me in. You're the best thing that's ever happened to me."

It was like all of the air had been sucked from the room; my throat constricted with emotion and tears lined my eyes. A buzzing high zipped through my body as happiness poured into my every limb.

Ethan King loved me.

I was loved. I was worthy and deserving of real love, something Bryce had made me forget.

He was high, sure, but that just made you tell the truth right? He fucking loved me.

"I love you too." My voice shook and Ethan grinned, a loopy grin that only one on drugs could give.

He looked down at his body, seemingly noticing all the pins and metal for the first time. "Why do I look like a robot?"

I laughed. "You shattered your femur and broke some ribs. They had to build everything with metal screws and plates, but you'll be okay."

He nodded, his eyes growing heavy. "That fucking car. People never look for motorcycles."

I stroked his hand. "I know. I'm sorry. Get some rest."

I didn't want to upset him by probing right now.

"Fuck that white SUV," Ethan mumbled before falling asleep.

White SUV.

White Range Rover SUV?

Chills broke out on my arms, and a deep knowing came over me. Bryce was sick in the head and he'd tried to kill my new boyfriend. I was sure of it now. I never should have doubted my intuition.

I was going to make him regret the fucking day he'd been born.

I had one more chance at a happily-ever-after and he wasn't going to ruin it for me.

Slipping out of the room, I told the nurse at the nurses' station I was going to send another friend back to sit with Ethan while I ran an errand.

Walking out to see the waiting room was empty but for James, I beelined it over to my new friend.

"Hey, you want to see him?" I tried to put a semi fake smile on, to mask the rage building inside of me.

"Yeah, you done? How is he?"

I nodded and held out my hand. "He's good, sedated but good. Can I borrow the car? I'm gonna grab him some flowers or something."

He wiped his eyes. "Sure. I'll sit with him until you get back."

I smiled. "Thanks, man. You want a coffee or anything?"

He shook his head. "I'm good. See you soon."

I clasped my fingers around the keys to the SUV and stormed out to the parking lot.

The second I got behind the wheel, I dialed Bryce's cell phone, which I still knew by heart. Would he still be in town? I had no idea, but if he was, I was going to interrogate the shit out of him. He picked up on the second ring.

"Called to apologize?" he answered.

I tamped down my rage. That would get me nowhere with him.

"Are you still in Flagstaff? I need to see you." I spoke through gritted teeth and started driving to the fanciest hotel in town: the Holiday Inn. I had no idea where he was staying, but I was going to inspect every inch of his bumper.

"Really?" Surprise littered his tone. "You want to see me…?"

"Yep," I lied. "Right now."

He tsk-tsked. "Well, darling, I'm glad to see you are coming around to things, but we left after your little felon meathead threatened me. Let's do dinner tomorrow night."

I had to take three deep breaths in and out. "You left right after? Like noon? Right after the lodge?"

"Ohh, the second person to interrogate me today. What's going on?" There was a smile in his voice, I could hear it. The police officer must have contacted him. I had to pull over to keep my shaking hands from crashing my car and joining Ethan in the hospital.

"Bryce, don't fuck with me. I know letting go of me has been hard on you, but did you hurt Et—?"

"You made a vow, you lying bitch. I'll fuck with you all I want. Stay away from that scumbag and I'll be happy." The line went dead.

I sat there in shock, staring at the screen for a full minute before screaming in frustration that I hadn't recorded that call. Did he just admit to hurting Ethan? Ohhh, I'd kill him! Technically he said he'd fuck with me, not Ethan, but ... oh my God, Bryce was beyond reason. Tears streamed down my cheeks as the desperation of my situation settled into me.

Stay away from that scumbag and I'll be happy.

"Fuck!" I pounded the steering wheel. My streaming tears turned to full-on sobs as a scream of rage ripped from my throat and I beat my hands across my thighs.

Bryce was controlling my happiness all over again. The first man in a long time that I truly cared about had just told me he loved me, and now I was going to have to leave him to keep him safe.

It wasn't fair.

Bryce was unhinged, but I couldn't see a way out. If I killed him outright, I went to jail. If I stayed with Ethan, he'd end up dead. I had to...

Stay away from that scumbag and I'll be happy.

Sobs racked my body as a panic attack set in. I'd have to leave Ethan. Move out and completely ghost him. If he thought I was doing this because of Bryce, he'd never let me go. I'd have to make it look real...

But could I? Could I leave the man I loved while he was injured and down on his luck? Was I capable of that? Even now I was aimlessly going to the blood sugar app on my phone and checking in on him.

I felt paralyzed. I didn't know what to do, so I sat there on the side of the road until James texted me and asked me when I was coming back. He said Ethan was asking for me.

I turned the car around and parked in the hospital lot. Checking myself in the mirror, I tried to dab at my eyes and make it look like I wasn't just crying. Walking felt like too much work at this point; my body had completely shut down at the thought of leaving Ethan in his time of need.

He'd just told me he loved me, that I was the best thing that ever happened to him. How could I leave him?

I wrestled with what to do all the way up to his

room. When I knocked and stepped in, James was sitting by his bed and Ethan looked up at me.

"Hailey," he breathed, "it's good to see you. I'm so sorry if I scared you."

I frowned and looked at James. He didn't remember seeing me earlier?

"Buddy, Hailey's already been in to see you," he told Ethan, and then looked at me. "Nurse said as the anesthesia wears off he might be repeating the same thing. Memory will be fuzzy."

Oh my God. It hit me like a Mack truck. He didn't remember confessing his love for me ... that I'd said it back.

Maybe it was better this way, maybe it was a sign from the universe. I could make a clean break before it got serious, before Bryce killed him.

"Hey." I moved towards the bed, my mind running a mile a minute as I tried to keep from crying. I hadn't even left yet and I was already mourning him.

I was one hundred-percent certain that Ethan was the love of my life ... and I was going to walk away to keep him safe.

THIRTEEN

The next month was hell. Absolute fucking hell. Bryce texted me every Friday night at 7PM. Always the same sentence. **How's Ethan?** Any cop would see it and think he was being caring, but I saw it for what it was: a threat. I never responded. Over the last month, I helped Ethan recover at home while he hobbled around the shop and tried to keep up with business. I couldn't leave him while he was down and injured, it just wasn't in me. But today he'd gotten his first cast off and moved into a less restrictive one without all of the pins and crazy stuff. He'd be more mobile, and he was off pain pills and just taking ibuprofen.

Today I could leave and not have the guilt gnaw at me for the rest of my life. He knew something was

weird with me, but hadn't really brought it up. He'd
ask me to sleep in his bed and I would decline and
say that I had homework or wanted to be alone. I was
trying to protect myself, keep my heart from falling
deeper in love with him.

Ethan was so lovable.

We'd never spoken about the accident and who
we thought did it. He chalked it up to a random hit
and run and I didn't want to put anything in his
head. James hadn't said a word either, and the police
had turned up no leads.

"Where is your head right now?" he asked me as
I played with my food at the dining table. I'd made
homemade lasagna, a final meal before I left him to
his own devices. I'd have to go back to the youth
hostel. I'd already booked my room for tonight. I just
needed to get the nerve to break up with him.

"Hailey?" he asked again.

Fuck.

"You've been so distant since my accident..." He
trailed off and suddenly I knew it was time. I had to
do this. Bryce had been radio silent lately except for
the weekly texts. But he'd done that before and then
he just showed up wherever I was.

I stood, letting my fork fall to my plate, and stared
at the corner of the wall. I had to make this look real or

he would never buy it. "Ethan … I've been thinking a lot since your accident. I don't think I'm ready for this kind of serious commitment. I just got out of a marriage and moved in with another guy. I need time to find myself and so I think it's best if I move out. If we break up."

Silence.

"You're not even going to look at me when you break up with me?" His voice was like gravel, and no matter how hard I tried to keep them back, the tears spilled onto my cheeks.

I flicked my eyes to his, figuring I at least owed him the common decency of eye contact, and quickly realized it was a mistake to look at him. There was so much emotion swirling behind those blue eyes it nearly knocked me over. Ethan stood, gripping the edge of the table to steady himself, and faced off with me.

"I'm in love with you," he declared for the second time, but to his knowledge only the first, and more tears leaked from my eyes. "If you want space, if you want to move out and try to go slower, I can totally do that, but I can't undo the fact that I've fallen madly in love with you."

A whimper left my throat as I gathered the courage to speak. "Ethan..." I stroked his cheek. "You saved me. I don't think you will ever know how much you pulled me up out of the darkness."

He clasped his hand over mine and smiled in a tortured way.

"But I don't love you back."

I went for the kill and wiped the smile off his face. "I'm just not ready for love right now and I think we should be friends."

The complete and utter shock that marred his features socked me right in the gut. He was not ready for this; he had *not* been expecting this.

"Okay..." He pulled back, looking hurt, looking livid.

I couldn't breathe. "I'm sorry."

Turning from the kitchen, I ran to my room and slammed the door. Hysteria slammed into me and I felt like I was making a huge mistake. But what if I told him I was leaving because I thought Bryce was going to hurt him if I didn't? He'd kill Bryce and end up in jail. If I stayed with him, Bryce would hurt Ethan and I'd never be able to live with myself. This was the only way.

I grabbed my bags, already having packed them before dinner, and looked at the bed. I'd left the bedding ... it was a gift and I didn't feel right keeping it. Especially since I didn't need bedding at the youth hostel.

Standing there, I tried to control my breathing, to get the tears to stop falling. I couldn't completely fall apart or he would wonder why this chick who didn't love him was losing her shit over him. Reaching out for my phone, I ordered an Uber. I must have stood there a full five minutes before I felt I was composed enough to leave the room, leave the man who'd given me hope, who'd given me love.

Peeling open the door, I stepped out and prepared myself for him to beg me to stay, to call me on my shit, but his bedroom door was shut and he wasn't there. Maybe it was better this way. Through blurry tears, I made my way down the stairs and outside. Once I used my key to close up the shop, I slipped the single key off my key ring and dropped it in the key-drop box. He'd find it there in the morning and figure out what it was for. I'd have to come back for my bike later. My possessions had ballooned to two large duffle bags and I couldn't carry them while riding my bike.

As the Uber pulled away to take me to the youth hostel, I got an alert on my phone. It was from the app that helped me monitor Ethan's blood sugar.

You've been removed from this account.

A sharp pang sliced through my chest reading those words. I don't know why, but him removing me from his account hurt me most of all.

It was over. We were over before we had really even begun.

What had I done?

Through blurry, enraged tears, I texted Bryce.

I broke up with Ethan.

Then I threw my phone on my lap and burst into tears as the Uber driver cast worried glances in the back seat.

Bryce's reply was immediate.

Good girl.

He'd won. I was trapped all over again and he'd won.

TWO WEEKS. It had been two weeks since I'd left Ethan, and a deep depression had settled into my bones. The few times Angela had tried to probe for more information about why I broke up with him, I just kept it vague. *"I can't do serious right now. I have issues,"* I'd told her.

I tried to keep busy with school, which was getting more challenging, and Angela and I hung out often, but she had a kid so there were many nights that I was alone. I hung late at the public library, or sat at a Starbucks studying, anything to keep from going back to the hostel. My new bunkmate's name was Frida, and she was a chatterbox. I needed to find my own place but couldn't yet afford it. I was still paying my way through school and I really didn't want to pay any student loans. I'd avoided Ethan for as long as I could, but today I'd have to go over there and get my bike. Taking Ubers everywhere was getting expensive, and I hated walking too far alone at night.

I had texted him right after I'd left class to see if I could come grab my bike in an hour and he'd replied with one word.

Sure.

After everything we'd been through together, we'd been reduced to one-word texts. It fucking broke my heart. I loved Ethan, and I wanted to keep him safe, but I also didn't want Bryce to be keeping me from happiness. Two weeks after that text I'd sent him about Ethan and I breaking up and I hadn't seen or heard anything. No Friday text of "How's Ethan?" No mysterious Louis Vuitton's, nothing. Maybe he just wanted me to be alone forever and then he'd back off.

"Next!" the lady at the student services window called, snapping me out of my stupor. I'd been paying my tuition in cash each semester and this semester's payment was due today. I'd just made enough tips from last night to cover it. Living at the hostel was more expensive than Ethan's, so I was going to have to work harder to make ends meet.

"Hey, I need to pay my tuition. Hailey Willows. Nursing." I set the stack of cash on the counter.

Her long purple and glitter fingernails typed away at the keyboard. This lady was new, I hadn't met her yet.

"Ma'am, you already paid." She gave me an annoyed look. "Next!" She shouted to someone behind me.

Alarm bells started going off as panic rushed through me. Fucking BRYCE!

I put out a hand to stop the next student from stepping forward and glared at the lady. "Who paid it? When?" I growled.

She raised one eyebrow as if to tell me not to sass her. "I'm sorry," I amended. "This is important. I have a stalker," I whispered. I figured a partial truth was best here.

Her features softened. "Three days ago. We don't keep record of who paid, but someone paid for the rest of your degree here."

Anger flushed through me. I wanted to fucking do this for myself! I wanted to pay my way through school and have something to be proud of at the end of it. Something I did for me. Bryce was relentless.

"Can you return it?"

Her eyes widened. "Girl, that's like five grand. You sure?"

I breathed in through my nose to calm myself. I, Hailey Willows, would become a nurse on my own. I would build a life for myself that Bryce in no way helped build.

"I'm positive. Can you?"

She nodded. "He paid with a card. I can return it to the card and make a note on the account to only accept in-person payments from Hailey Willows. We are going to have to ask for ID from now on in that case."

Relief flooded through me and I reached out and grasped her hand. "Oh my God. Thank you. That's fine."

She patted my hand and nodded. "I had a stalker once. Left his dirty undies in my car, so I get it."

Yeah, not really the same thing, but I nodded anyway, because, Sisterhood.

"Alright, Mrs. Willows, that will be $1083 for this semester, and I'm going to need to see some ID." She winked.

Ouch. Handing over a grand in my current financial position was tough, but I was a survivor. I'd proven that to myself. I was going to do this on my own and Bryce could shove his credit card up his ass.

AFTER PAYING MY TUITION, I took the light rail downtown and started to walk the five minutes to Ethan's place.

Almost at your place. I texted him a heads-up in case he was with a client or working on a bike.

The weather was amazing and reminded me why I loved Arizona. Our winters were mild and incredible. It gave me time to try and calm my nerves and prepare to see Ethan. With our history together growing up, and after sharing intimate moments, it would make it hard to ever be "friends." It was all or nothing and I'd chosen nothing, so I didn't expect him to be all chummy with me. Most likely we'd exchange comments about the weather and he'd give me my bike and tell me to have a nice day. I'd want to ask him all about how his diabetes was and his leg and what was happening in the *Jessica Jones* show we had been watching together, but I wouldn't. I had to seem like I didn't love him. Especially since Bryce was still around and trying to woo me back with his stupid credit card bullshit.

As I walked up to the shop I noticed the garage bay doors were down, which they never were during business hours. My bike was on its kickstand out front, and Sebastian, the shop manager, was standing next to it.

Shit.

Desperation gripped me as I realized Ethan didn't even want to see me. He'd fucking closed the doors and sent Sebastian to deal with me. Oh God.

Tears welled in my eyes and I forced them to move backwards and go into my head. I could not cry right now.

"Hey..." My voice shook.

"Hey." Sebastian's voice was short and clipped.

He hated me.

Oh my God, I hadn't thought this through. About how I'd be hurting Ethan and how his friends would turn on me.

Sebastian handed my bike to me and I mumbled a thanks.

When he turned to walk away, I called out to him.

"How is Ethan?" I nearly whimpered.

He had one hand on the door, looking over his shoulder at me with disgust. "You wrecked him."

Then he walked inside and slammed the door.

Wrecked.

I wrecked Ethan. I, Hailey 2.0, was a fucking wrecker. How had this happened? *Ethan saves me and I break him?* I couldn't deal with that. I wasn't okay with that. Hopping on my bike, I rode off down the street, tears streaming down my face as I peddled harder and harder, unsure where I was going. I must have looked like a mad woman, openly crying as I passed people in the streets on my bike. I didn't care. I'd fucking wrecked Ethan King and nothing else mattered.

I didn't know that I had been slowly gravitating towards the cemetery until I reached the gates.

Mom.

I hadn't thought about my mother in a long time. It was easier that way. She wasn't mother of the year, but she was the only one I had and she loved me fiercely. She'd been lost to a drug addiction, but I never held that against her. She was weak-willed and she'd done her best. Just like I was doing now. My god damn best. Navigating this shit with Bryce alone was wearing on me. I popped off my bike and walked it into the gates, turning right at the entrance.

I'd only been here a couple times, and yet I knew the path right to her grave. I'd committed it to memory. When poor people die, there is no funeral, no fancy granite headstone or procession of limos. The state put you in a cement grave and stuck a two-inch nameplate on a stick and that was it. That was all my mom got.

When I reached her final resting place, I propped my bike on its kickstand and fell to my knees.

Gloria Willows. 1977-2013

Thirty-six. She had only been given thirty-six years before life chewed her up and spit her out. She'd had me already by the age I was now.

The cemetery only had a few people and they were pretty far away, so I just started to talk. I talked to my mom like she was still alive and caught her up on all she'd missed. Me going to live with the foster family, going off to private school and meeting Bryce. Getting married at eighteen and living through hell in that marriage. Meeting Ethan. Everything. I laughed and cried and it felt like a five hundred pound weight had been lifted off of me. I realized then how much it had been killing me not to tell anyone about why I'd really broken up with Ethan. How I was still in love with him and only wanted to protect him.

When I was done sharing my life story with my mom, I just sat there peacefully, breathing, before finally deciding to head back to the hostel. I was just standing to leave, noticing it was getting dark outside, when my phone buzzed with a text.

It was from Bryce. I almost didn't want to read it but that fucker had a way of pulling me in. What if it was about Ethan?

What kind of stupid girl refunds her paid college tuition? Clearly not smart enough to go to college. PS How is your mom?

The college shit I expected. His comments about me being stupid rolled right off me. But the mom thing ... that made chills break out on my arms. I spun around, looking left and then right, but there was no one here. Other than one car, an older black Honda Civic that was driving away.

He was having me followed.

I decided to poke the bear. Fuck Bryce.

What kind of pathetic limp dick guy needs to stalk his ex and try to buy her back with money?

The second I sent it, I felt vindicated. I'd never spoken to him like that before and it felt so good.

I always faked it with you. You suck in bed, I fired off.

I sent another: **I can't even divorce you in peace. You have to follow me out to Phoenix like a puppy.**

I went for the kill: **I felt more for Ethan in our few months together than I did for you in our entire marriage.**

"Fuck you Bryce!" I screamed to the empty cemetery, imagining my mom giving me a fist bump across the dinner table like she would when I would get an A on my report card.

When his reply came back, I glanced down at my phone.

Oh you're going to regret that.

Shit. Maybe I'd taken the Bryce bashing too far? It was getting dark, and considering he was somehow watching me, I'd better get on my bike and get the hell out of here. Normally when I was scared, I could call Ethan, but I'd burned that bridge. Next would be Angela but she had her kid.

I was alone. For the first time since leaving Ethan, I truly felt alone. An odd sense of calmness washed over me. I'd cut off Ethan so Bryce wouldn't hurt him anymore. My mom was dead and I didn't know who my father was. There was literally no one left in this world that Bryce could hurt to get to me. If he hurt me, I would deal with it and that was okay, but he couldn't threaten me anymore. I wasn't going to live in fear. I was free and I was going to enjoy that freedom as best I could.

I peddled quickly with cautious glances over my shoulder, but I didn't expect Bryce to retaliate right away. That wasn't his style. No, he would sit on it, plan it out, and then come after me. When he did, I'd be ready.

THE VERY NEXT DAY, I decided to take matters into my own hands. It was Angela's idea and I was stoked for it.

"Hi, I'd like to sign up for a class?" I told the lady behind the desk.

She looked me up and down. "You?"

Okay, I wasn't exactly buff, but that didn't mean I was out of shape. "Yes. Me. Krav Maga."

My eyes flicked over to the gym mat behind her, where a six-foot-tall dude was taking another dude to the ground and I grinned. I'd love to lay Bryce out on his ass the next time he tried to touch me.

She held her hands up. "Okay. You got it. Our women's class meets every Monday night and it's twenty bucks a class."

Eighty bucks a month? Ouch. I'd have to figure it out.

I nodded. "That's perfect."

I'd come to terms with how things were going to end. It was either going to be me in a body bag or Bryce in jail. I was hoping for the latter.

FOURTEEN

The next week stretched on and suddenly it was Christmas Eve. I'd gone to approximately one Krav Maga class and had fallen in love. The thrill of knocking a toy plastic gun out of a big chick's hand and watching it fall to the floor had filled me with a total adrenaline rush. Bryce was radio silent again, which was fine by me, but Ethan was the one who had my every waking thought. *How is he? Does he miss me? Is he dating someone else?* He and his boys never came in to Mickey's when I was on shift. It was like they called ahead and asked who was working.

"Girl, you look adorable!" Angela shrieked, and I spun around to hug my friend. We were working tonight and I was just putting on my Santa hat to go with my little red dress I'd found, and knee high black boots. I looked absolutely fuckable tonight, with no one to fuck. It was depressing, really.

"Thanks, girl. How's Finn?"

Her son had an ear infection last time I checked.

She waved a hand. "Gave him that pink shit and now he's all better."

I laughed. "They still give that?" I remembered that pink shit from when I was little.

"Yep. Remember when we were in third grade and we got lice?"

I chuckled. "My mom threatened to shave my head."

She grinned. "They still use that stinky stuff and that tiny comb too."

Her talk of our childhood made me smile. I didn't have that in L.A. I didn't have a home there or anyone from my past, and it had made me forget a part of myself.

"Girl, that dress barely covers your hoo-ha. You trying to get extra tips?" Her eyes fell to my crotch and laughter pealed out of me.

"Maybe." I winked. Showing some skin was good for business; there was no shame in my game.

She winked and gave me a hip bump.

We walked out to our shift with smiles on our

faces. The holidays were here, and although I didn't have a family to spend it with, it was good to be among friends. Angela was spending tomorrow with her son and her parents. She'd invited me, but I didn't want to crash. Tomorrow night there was actually a "Singles On Christmas" event in Phoenix I thought about going to.

If I were still in L.A., I'd be up at 4AM Christmas morning, cooking lunch for Bryce and his friends and then off to the clubhouse for dinner with his parents. I'd be a stressed-out, overworked robot with not a shred of happiness. This year wasn't perfect, but my first Christmas free of Bryce, doing whatever I wanted and not cooking for a dozen ungrateful idiots, sounded perfect.

Mickey greeted me and Angela: "Grab me a Heineken, dollface?"

Angela handed him one and he nodded, popping the top off and handing it to a customer behind the bar.

"Thanks for coming in last minute. We're slammed!" he told me.

I smiled. "You know me! I love the extra hours."

We settled into our routine. I had the left side of the bar, Angela had the right, and Taylor scooped up the middle. For a night when people were usually with family or at Mass, there sure were a lot of people in the bar. People were tipping back beers like it was water and tips were flowing freely.

"Holidays are the best!" Angela told me on our fifteen-minute break out back.

I nodded. "Hell yeah they are." I had a fat stack of cash in my pocket that was going to pay for these expensive Krav Maga classes.

"You gotta find a proper place to live, mama. You can't be living in a youth hostel all through college. It ain't right." She was extra Latina tonight and it made me smile.

I chuckled. "It's all I can afford." Marina, the youth hostel owner, lowered my rate since I had stayed long term. It was now three hundred a month. A bit more than I paid Ethan, but that was a charity case anyway.

Angela shook her head. "No, girl. We'll find you a place. Like a room on Craigslist. Somewhere I can visit and not have that chatty bitch all up in our faces."

I chuckled. "She's going back to Germany. I'll have a new roommate next week."

Angela did her *whatever* thing and we carried on with the easy banter. I loved that I could be myself around Angela. I could talk about being broke without being embarrassed; I could talk about Bryce and my hopes and dream or fears and know she wasn't judging.

Mickey poked his head out. "Can you wrap it up? We just had two six-tops come in."

Technically, we still had five minutes left, but Mickey was the best boss in the world, so with a sigh we stood and went back inside.

The moment my eyes landed on the new people who'd just sat in my section, my gut clenched and the air knocked out of me.

Ethan.

It felt like I hadn't seen him in forever. Weeks. And there he was, looking amazing in a black button-down shirt and dress slacks. Jesus, I forgot how handsome he was. My eyes flicked to his foot to see it was in a walking boot. That meant he was probably doing well in physical therapy.

I couldn't breathe. I had to remind myself to breathe, that's how affected I was in seeing him again.

"Want to switch?" Angela whispered beside me.

No way. I needed to talk to Ethan, even though it would torture me.

I shook my head. "I got this."

My eyes ran over the rest of the people at his

table and I noticed for the first time that there was a girl next to him. A beautiful, if you like trashy, blonde. Sebastian, James, and two other girls were there too.

Three girls. Three guys.

It was a fucking group date.

Maybe I should have Angela take it. Fuck, he's turning around.

I forced myself to put on a smile and walk towards the table just as Ethan caught sight of me.

His mouth popped open in surprise a little, and then his eyes flicked to my knee-high boots and slowly dragged up my body, pausing for a moment at my thighs. His jaw ticked and he leaned into Sebastian to say something. I saw Sebastian mouth "Sorry" and then I was at the table.

Ethan didn't know I was working tonight. He was actively avoiding me and that stung.

"Merry Christmas." My voice shook and sounded way more timid than I'd meant.

"Merry Christmas," Sebastian answered in monotone as Ethan pulled his gaze from me to his date, giving me his back.

A bomb went off in my chest as I realized I'd let the only man I ever really loved go, and now he was free to fall in love with another ... while he still owned my heart.

"What can I get you?" I mumbled, never taking my eyes off Ethan. I was just staring at his back like a psycho while the table rambled off their orders and I scribbled them down. I didn't trust myself to remember anything right now.

It was Ethan's turn. "Ethan?" His name on my lips made my belly warm. "What can I get you tonight?"

His date's eyes snapped up to mine the moment I said his name, but she kept quiet.

Slowly, he turned in his chair and faced me. What I saw on his face shocked me ... there was so much anger. I'd hurt him more than I realized. My intention had been to keep him safe and I'd done the opposite.

"You can have Angela get me a Bud Light," he growled, and gave me his back again, causing his blond bimbo date to burst into laughter.

Tears swelled in my eyes, but I turned before they fell.

He had every right to be mad at me. I'd left him when he was injured and down on his luck. He told me he loved me, a vulnerable thing for a man to do, and I told him I didn't feel the same.

237

Weaving in and out of the packed bar and over to Angela, I handed her the order slip. "Actually let's switch."

She gave me a sympathetic look and nodded.

Over the next hour, every five minutes or so my traitorous eyes kept flicking over to Ethan. He kept playing with that bitch's blond hair, or her necklace, or she'd touch his arm. They were fucking flirting so bad they were seconds away from making a baby and it made me livid. Not once did I catch Ethan looking at me. Not once. I was dead to him and that killed me.

My phone buzzed and I pulled up a text from "Psycho Ex," as I'd lovingly named Bryce's number.

I miss your sweet potato casserole.

I growled in frustration at the delusional world this man was living in.

Fuck off and die. You're Blocked.

I texted back and then blocked his number. Something I should have done ages ago. Part of me feared blocking him wouldn't allow me to keep tabs on him, but really he was keeping tabs on me and I was sick of hearing from him.

I was so frustrated with Ethan and Bryce and the whole world that when I spun with four beers in my hands I didn't realize until it was too late. I stepped right into the pathway of the bathroom and crashed into Ethan. Beers crashed to the floor and shattered at my feet. We were smashed up against one another, broken beer glass all around us.

"Fuck!" I yelled, tears streaming down my face as I looked up to stare into his blue eyes. The anger was gone and something had replaced it.

Sympathy.

"This is becoming your signature move," he said, keeping his rock hard body pressed against mine even though he could step backward if he wanted.

It was something the old funny Ethan would say; I laughed while tears streamed down my face, because I was a fucking mess. My body, pressed against his, felt so good I didn't want to let go, but I had to. Pulling back, I gave him a weak smile. I couldn't stop crying. What an idiot I must look like. Tears just flowed down my face and I couldn't look him in the eye.

"I'm so sorry." I pinned my gaze at his feet watching the broken glass and liquid spill out onto the floor.

He wiped a tear from my cheek and I finally met his electric blue eyes. "Me too. Goodbye, Hailey."

Then he walked away, crunching glass as he went.

It felt like goodbye, like goodbye forever. That felt like closure and it shocked the shit out of me. I wasn't ready to let Ethan go. I didn't want closure. I didn't care what Bryce did to me, I'd warn Ethan about him and let him make his own decision, but I couldn't live without him knowing how I really felt. I needed to tell him that I loved him back.

I ran over to the bar. "Mickey, family emergency, can I get cut early?"

He gave me a look, but then scanned the bar, which was slowly emptying out. "Alright, doll. Thanks for your help tonight."

I nodded and quickly ran to grab the broom and dustbin. With ninja skills I mopped that glass up in record time and put the "wet floor caution" sign out after I was done.

Then I ran to Angela, handing her the four beers I was supposed to drop at her table.

"Angela, I'm cut. Wrap up my station?" I asked her, trying to work as fast as I could.

She nodded, taking the beers from me. "Merry Christmas!"

"Merry Christmas!" I replied, running into the back room to clock out and drop off my apron. I was gone all of three minutes, and when I returned and ran up to Ethan's table to declare my undying love, he was gone. His friends too.

No!

Calling up an Uber, I paced the sidewalk as I waited the four agonizing minutes for it to get there. Where was Ethan headed tonight? It was 1 AM on Christmas. Probably home. Probably home with his date to...

No.

When I got in the Uber, I barked off the address and told him to drive like this was the fucking *Amazing Race*. He did not disappoint. Speeding through downtown, he deposited me on Ethan's doorstep in record time. There was a Mustang in the driveway and I didn't know whose car that was, but I hoped he was home.

"Thanks!" I watched him drive off and decided that if Ethan wasn't home, I would sit on his doorstep and wait all night if I had to. He might be too angry to forgive me, or he might have moved on, but I couldn't live with myself if I didn't tell him the truth.

Without overthinking it, I stepped up to the door and the sound of rock music blared out from behind it. Reaching my fist back, I banged on the door like a cop and the music turned off. Then it wrenched open and Ethan was standing there, eyes narrowed.

"Hailey?"

"Who is it?" A blond head peeped up behind him and looked down at me.

Now or never. Otherwise I'd live with this regret my entire life.

My throat constricted as I tried to keep from crying. "I lied." I looked him right in the eyes. "I'm in love with you. I've always been in love you. I lied to keep you safe because Bryce is the one that hit you with his car and he's been taunting me to break up with you ever since."

There I said it. The words rushed out of me and then the silent tears fell from my eyes in thin rivulets and down my cheeks.

"What the *fuck* is going on?" Blondie asked Ethan.

He was staring at me with an unreadable gaze, chest rising and falling. Finally he turned to the girl. "I think you should go home. We're done."

Her eyebrows hit her hairline and hope bloomed in my chest.

"Excuse me?"

Ethan stepped back, opening the door wider. "Leave," he commanded, and I tried to wipe the grin off my face, with no success. She disappeared for a second and then returned with her purse and keys.

"Asshole!" she called out behind her as she blasted past me.

Without a word, Ethan stepped back and I walked in to the small front office of his shop. When he closed the door behind me, he locked it and then stood before me. His gaze was now molten, glowing. "Say it again."

I nodded. He needed all the facts, the entire story. "So Bryce drives a white car and when you came out of anesthesia you said a white car. Then when I called him—"

He put a finger to my lips, sending chills down my spine. "No. I'll deal with that later. Say the other part again."

A grin pulled at my lips. "Ethan King ... I'm fucking in love with you. Deeply. Hopelessly in love with you-" This time he cut my words off with a kiss. Stepping forward, his entire body pressed against mine as his lips crashed into me. There was a hunger in his kiss that I matched. I wanted him so badly I whimpered. I never thought I'd have this with him again, and joy spread throughout my limbs, but it quickly turned to a throbbing desire. Pushing me backward, he pressed me up against the wall, pushing his hardness into me.

Fuck me.

MY BELLY DROPPED as heat pulsed between my legs, making me slick. I opened my mouth, allowing his tongue to go further in and glide with mine. Reaching out, I pulled his shirt over his head, hating the two seconds where he had to stop kissing me.

My dress was a full snap front and Ethan made every use of that feature now. In one swift pull, he ripped the front of my tight red dress open, freeing my breasts. I was braless, and when his head scooped down to take my nipple in his mouth, I started to fumble with his belt. We both shared an urgent need to consume each other, to make our love known in physical ways.

"I need you. Now," I panted as his hand slipped into my underwear and started to massage my most delicate spot.

He pulled back to look at me with a steely gaze. "Now?" He slipped one finger and plunged it inside of me. "Here?" He leaned forward and trailed his tongue along my left nipple.

Jesus fuck. "Yes!" I shouted, letting my dress fall

to the floor so that I was only standing there in a black lace thong and knee-high boots. My Santa hat had fallen off somewhere near the door.

Ethan backed away from me, never letting his eyes go from my body, and pulled his pants and boxers off. Stepping forward, I reached out and grabbed his hardness, relishing the moan that left his throat. Stroking him, I watched him as he fumbled for his wallet and pulled out a condom.

It wasn't a ski cabin in the snow, there was no champagne, and I might qualify as a hooker if I kept these boots on, but I didn't care. I wanted all of Ethan and I wanted him now. He rolled on the condom as I stepped out of my panties, then he reached around with two firm hands on my ass and lifted me up. When he lowered me on top of him and slowly plunged inside of me, I cried out and rocked my hips into him, deepening our movements. Deep pleasure burst inside of me as he walked with me riding him in the air, setting me on top of the glass counter he used to check out customers.

I was fucking the love of my life on a counter in a motorcycle shop while wearing knee high boots ... and I didn't care. It was perfect; pure passion. As his hips rocked into mine, a pleasurable tingle started to spread throughout my legs and I threaded my fingers through his hair. Dipping his head down, he took my nipple into his mouth and ran his tongue over the bud.

Holy fuck, that felt good.

With the counter supporting my weight, and my legs draped up over his shoulders, Ethan dipped his free hand between us and started to work on me with his thumb.

"Jesus Christ!" I screamed as an orgasm came out of nowhere and took me in her clutches. Electric tingles shot up my spine as I arched my back and threw my head forward, biting down on his shoulder lightly. Ethan rocked with me, using my motions to pleasure himself as I became slicker and slicker.

He finally cried out, moaning, and then all of his muscles tightened as I spun my hips in a circular motion to please him. By the time we'd stopped, we were both glossy with sweat, panting and grinning at each other like fools.

"Did we just fuck on your check-out counter?" I asked.

He smirked. "Are you still wearing your boots?" He looked at my naked form draped across his counter, booted feet dangling off.

We both laughed, and he reached his arms

around me, picking me up and depositing me on the floor, where I could stand on my own two feet.

I just stood there, naked, panting, exposed.

Reaching up, he wiped the hair away from my face. "God, Hailey. I missed you so much it hurt."

My heart pinched and I laced my fingers through his. "That was the hardest thing I have ever done. But I just wanted to protect you."

His face clouded over, eyes sharpening. "About that ... I'm going to need you to tell me where Bryce works. It's time I pay that motherfucker a visit."

Oh shit.

FIFTEEN

"Ethan, you can't! This is why I didn't want to tell you."

Ethan was pacing the kitchen in his walking boot and I wondered how he'd had the strength to do all we did downstairs with that thing on.

"Hailey, this has gone far enough. I'm just going to make him see that fucking with me is the wrong idea. That even looking at you is a mistake."

I sighed. "Ethan, you're going to beat the shit out of him and end up in jail. On Christmas Eve!" I shouted the last part.

He shrugged as if to say "so what?" "Then call my lawyer!"

I stood and padded over to where he paced, planting myself before him and forcing him to stop and look at me. "Ethan, it's Christmas Eve, my first holiday on my own, and all I want is to fall asleep next to you and wake up with you still there." I laid my cards on the table, hating how vulnerable it made me.

He sighed, looking defeated. "That's the cutest fucking thing you've ever said to me."

I grinned, slipping my arms around his waist and tucking my head into his neck, breathing him in. I never wanted to be away from him again.

Pulling back to look at me, he smirked. "Let's go get your stuff out of that shithole. You're moving back in with me."

A grin pulled at the edges of my mouth. "Best Christmas present ever."

But something stormy crossed his face. "When you fake broke up with me, you said some very real shit. Like, you didn't want to move so fast after being married, and I just want you to know we can keep things light and slow. You can keep your room, turn it into a she-cave or whatever, and we'll just go at your pace."

Laughter bubbled out of me. "She-cave?"

He grinned. "Yeah, paint the walls pink and fill it with steamy romance novels or whatever you want. I don't care."

What did I do to deserve this man? My smile grew wider. "I love you," I told him, running my fingers through his hair. "That sounds perfect, but no need to go slow, I promise."

That night, as we lay down to sleep, I felt truly content for the first time in my life. This was what a stable relationship was like? I'd been missing out. With a smile on my lips and my head on Ethan's chest, I fell asleep.

I awoke to the smell of … cookies. Peeling my eyes open, I inhaled the scent of sugar cookies and my stomach rumbled. Padding into Ethan's bathroom, I brushed my teeth quickly with my toothbrush I set there the night before and then went out to see who was making this amazing smell.

In the kitchen, hunched over the stove, was a shirtless Ethan. On the counter were about five dozen sugar cookies.

"What in the name of diabetes is going on here?"

He spun, chuckling. "They're not for me. Every year, the Kings host a cookie decorating party. It's a blast, and someone usually ends up blackout drunk in your room, so fair warning."

Letting him pull me into his arms, I popped on my tiptoes and claimed his mouth in a hot kiss.

"Merry Christmas," I whispered after I pulled away.

"Merry Christmas."

"When is the party?" I rubbed my hands together. I was the queen of parties; this party would be my bitch.

I fucking loved Christmas. Reindeer, powdered sugar, Santa, caroling. All of it. Loved it.

A sly grin pulled at the edges of his mouth, dipping his finger into a bowl of powdered sugar he ran it across my lips. "We have time." Leaning forward, he sucked my bottom lip into his mouth and I moaned as the promise of pleasure was given to me.

"How much time?" I whispered back, allowing my tongue to drag across his neck.

"Like two hours," he panted.

I pulled back. "Two hours! To host a party? How many people? Are you supposed to serve food? What do you want me to make?" I threw open the fridge and cringed at the beer and deli meats. "Do you have fine china by any chance?"

"Why, yes, Santa, I did want blue balls for Christmas and for my girlfriend to turn into Martha Stewart."

I spun around, laughing. Shit, I'd gone all Hailey 1.0. Bryce had trained me like a dog on how to throw parties and I needed at least four hours to cook anything decent. But Ethan wasn't like that. These blobby cookies were proof of that.

"Sorry. Old life crept in on me." I closed the fridge and walked seductively across the room. "Did you just call me your girlfriend?" I trailed a finger across his chest.

He nodded. "Yep. Feeling confident, didn't even ask."

I laughed again. He was funny, I loved that about him. "Well, *boyfriend*, we've got two hours. What do you want to do?"

I glanced at the clock to find I'd slept until 10AM, so the party must be at noon. I was trying not to freak out about everything that needed to be done. Hailey 2.0 didn't give a shit; she fucked guys on checkout counters.

"Well..." He trailed a finger across my shoulder peeling the strap down. "I can think of a few things."

As his lips trailed down my neck, I moaned, but he quickly pulled away.

"But first I have to give you your present." He looked like a giddy schoolboy, eyes alight.

I frowned. "Hey, who is giving who blue balls now?"

He ran into the bedroom and returned with a small brown box. No label.

My heart fell. "Ethan, I didn't get you anything, I didn't think—"

He waved his hand. "I just want you, and I got that. Besides, I was supposed to give you this at the cabin but ... that didn't work out."

No. It didn't.

"Alright, but I'm getting you something really amazing for Valentine's Day."

He grinned. "Deal."

With that, I tore open the box and my eyes widened as I took the small pistol into my hands.

Ethan placed two gentle hands on each side of my shoulders. "I never want you to feel unsafe. Ever."

Tears welled in my eyes as I tried to keep my emotions in check. Ethan knew what it was like to live in an abusive relationship; his own mother had done it. She was still in it. He knew I was constantly looking over my shoulder for Bryce, and this gift meant more than I could ever say.

I grinned. "Thank you. By the way, I signed up for Krav Maga, so I'll be able to kick your ass in no time."

A smirk pulled at his lips. He took the gun from me and set it back in the box. "Oh really?"

With that he reached out lightning-quick and scooped me over his shoulder. A peal of laughter escaped me as he carried me to his bedroom.

I just kept thinking ... *this is happiness. This is what normal is like.*

As he laid me on the bed, I looked up at him. Messy hair, sultry blazing blue eyes. Ethan King was my fantasy. He took his fingers and started to trail them up my thighs.

"So..." When he got to my undies, he began to pull them down, and pleasure bloomed between my legs in anticipation.

Then the doorbell rang.

Ethan frowned. "Fuck it. They'll go away."

It rang again. And again. Like a teenager was going to town on it.

Anger flashed across his features and he picked up his phone. "I'll check the security cameras." He tapped at his phone. "It's some delivery-looking guy, but I don't see a package. Be right back."

He left the room and a stone sank in my stomach. I don't know why but I just felt like something was ... off. Who delivered shit on Christmas? Pulling back on my underwear, I trailed after him, my oversized t-shirt barely covering my ass.

"Be careful!" I shouted to him.

He was already downstairs and I was trying to catch up. Did Bryce know I was here? Did he send a hit man? I was completely paranoid.

Ethan nodded and then opened the door cautiously. "What the fuck, bro? It's Christmas and you're ringing my door bell like a cop," I heard him say just as I peered over his shoulder to see a man in a delivery outfit. I wasn't concerned with the guy, no, my eyes went behind him to what was on his truck.

My Audi.

With the slight scrape of the left rim when I'd curbed it at a Starbucks drive through. That was the last time Bryce hit me. Over scraping my rim by accident.

"Sorry, man. This guy paid me a thousand bucks to make sure his girl gets her car today. Even left her a note."

Ethan looked confused for a second.

"It's from Bryce," I croaked.

Ethan's gaze sharpened on the man. "Return the vehicle. It was sent by her stalker."

The guy paled. "What? I got no return address, man. I can't return it."

"Give me the note," I rasped—he'd said there was a note.

The guy slowly pulled a thick white card from under his clipboard. With shaking hands, I opened it and allowed Ethan to read over my shoulder.

Merry Christmas. I miss your cranberry stuffing. Please come home.

-B

I stood there at a complete and total loss for words.

What the actual fuck was going on? How did Bryce know I was here? Why the hell did he think sending me this was okay? He was more mentally ill than I previously thought.

Ethan turned to me slowly. "Hailey, I want you to call the police. From now on we are going to report everything."

I frowned. "It's Christmas, your party is in two hours."

"Call the police please," he told me, and slipped outside to talk to the guy, shutting the door behind him.

I sighed. This was not how I wanted to spend my first Christmas with Ethan, and somehow I think Bryce planned that. He was watching my every move.

"I THINK that's about all, ma'am. Sorry we couldn't be of more help." The officer tipped his hat in my direction.

After I'd called the police, I'd bolted upstairs to put some clothes on and slick my hair into a ponytail. Even going as far as throwing on some red lipstick and mascara. I'd wanted to look decent for the police statement.

"Thank you, Officers."

Ethan and I walked the policemen out while I replayed their reaction to my statement in my head.

They'd looked incredulously at me. "Your ex-husband is trying to give you your Audi back that you lost in the divorce, and you don't want it?"

"He was abusive. She wants nothing to do with him," Ethan had interjected on my behalf.

Understanding had dawned on their eyes, but then they'd asked the inevitable. Did I file a report on the abuse? Take pictures? Without any of that I couldn't get a restraining order. They told me the best I could do would be to send him a strongly-worded email that made it clear I did not want any more gifts or contact, and if he kept doing it, then they could consider stalking charges.

As I watched them drive away, I looked at my watch and then at Ethan. "People will be here in fifteen minutes," I told Ethan, who shut the door and sighed. "Let's put this entire thing behind us. I just want to forget about it. Christmas is my favorite holiday."

"I want to kill him," he said in a stone cold voice that made chills run the length of my arms.

I wanted Bryce gone too, but not at the expense of putting Ethan in prison. But clearly Bryce wasn't taking no for an answer. Like, what the fuck else did I need to do to get him to understand I was never going back to him?

I was tempted to unblock his number and see if he was texting me, but I pushed that aside. That's how he won, by taking space inside my head and captivating my thoughts, my time with Ethan.

I changed the subject: "Please tell me this party is potluck and all you were supposed to prepare were those cookies."

Ethan grinned. "It's potluck. All I was supposed to prepare were the cookies and the honey baked ham."

My eyes widened. "A ham! In fifteen minutes!"

Laughter burst from him as he reached out and

pulled me in his arms. "I'm kidding. Cookies and salad. That's it."

He knew how to rile me up and lighten the mood. I reached my arms around his waist, feeling the glucose monitor there. Memory of the hurt I'd felt when he took me off his account flushed through me. "I want one more gift from you for Christmas," I told him, and grabbed his phone. "Put me back on your account."

He chuckled, dark hair falling across his forehead. "Promise not to neurotically check it every ten minutes?"

I held up three fingers in my best Girl Scouts honor pose. "Only every twenty minutes."

We both smiled.

It wasn't an ideal Christmas, but all that mattered was that we were together.

THE NEXT DAY, I kept reflecting on the Audi delivery and what I could do to get through to Bryce that he needed to move on. The party had been a blast. Very chill, everyone low key; I won the cookie decorating challenge. No one else had thought to make a piping bag out of a zip lock baggie. Ethan must have texted the boys that I'd broken up with him to protect him from Bryce, because they were all super nice to me. Sebastian actually apologized for his previous chilly demeanor from when I'd come to collect my bike. All was forgiven and life felt pretty good. Except for the fact that Bryce wouldn't let me go... I needed to do something about that.

I decided the best I could do would be to write him a long email like the police had suggested. Something that I could later show police if necessary.

As I sat down to type the letter in my she-cave, which was now littered with study note cards and textbooks, I took a deep, cleansing breath.

This was my last ditch attempt to make him see reason before I let Ethan and his boys go give Bryce a scare like they'd been begging me to.

Dear Bryce,

When I met you in the hall between 3rd and 4th period, it was like time stopped. The rich and popular Bryce Conner was talking to me. Flirting with me. I felt so important, so treasured and loved. Little did I know that was all for show. You kept your demons locked inside of you until I married you and it was too late. I'm not sure that you've ever really loved me, because you don't know what unconditional love is. You don't know what a healthy relationship is. I'm *writing this letter to say that the first time you struck me, it fractured my soul. When someone you love and trust does something so vile, it breaks you. After my mother died, you became my family. I put every ounce of trust in you that I had and you broke it. You made me fear you, you made me hate you. Your controlling nature and delusional personality have finally led you astray.*

Bryce. We are Divorced.

I am NOT your wife anymore. I want nothing to do with you. EVER.

Please stop sending me gifts, texting me scary things, having me followed, having my new boyfriend followed. My life is without you now and I'm done communicating with you. If you send me anything again, I'm going to have to go to the police and file stalking charges. Your money can't hide you from that.

I hope you can get the help you need.

Have a nice life.

Bye.

Hailey Willows

Tears leaked down my cheeks as I read the letter. It was liberating to let all of that out and know that he would read it. With one final cleansing breath, I hit send and let it go. From now on I wasn't taking any more shit from Bryce. His next attempt to even send me a water bottle would be logged with the police.

After the email, I settled in for a long night of studying, only checking the app that monitored Ethan's blood sugar every hour. Okay, maybe every half hour.

By the time I woke in the morning I was feeling optimistic about life. My phone and email revealed no response from Bryce, but I knew he'd read the email. He wouldn't ever let an email from me go unread, but I'd also checked the "read request" notification box and was now one-hundred-percent certain he had got my message.

I was free of him, and if he tried anything again, it looked like I had good grounds for getting a restraining order with stalking charges.

As I padded out to the kitchen, I smiled at the array of fresh fruits and yogurt Ethan had laid on the table. "I missed you last night," he told me while scrambling eggs.

I came up behind him and let my hands stroke his chest, kissing him on the neck.

"Cram session for school." I'd slept in my she-cave.

"Over Christmas break?" he queried, scooping the eggs onto his plate and then some for me.

I nodded, popping a grape into my mouth. "Nursing students don't sleep. Get used to it." I winked.

He chuckled and then put his hand on a package that sat at the window sill.

"What's that?" I chewed a chunk of cantaloupe.

He tapped the box. "James dropped it off. It's a magnetic GPS tracking device for a car."

My eyebrows shot up. "Are you going to put it on my bike or something?"

He laughed. "That's a good idea. But no. I'm going to put it on Bryce's car. If he knows where we are, why shouldn't we always know where he is?"

Chills ran down my back. "Ethan..." I'd just declared myself done with Bryce drama.

"I just need you to tell me his license plate number and where he works." He asked casually, but there was nothing casual in his body language. He was filled with rage, muscles taut, gorilla ready to pounce.

"This doesn't sound legal and I don't want you and the guys jumping him and ending up in jail."

He put his hands up in a defensive gesture. "As

long as he stays away from you and me, I'm not going to do anything to him. I promise."

I sighed, putting my head in my hands. Track Bryce? That might actually be a good idea. The next time we wanted to go skiing I wouldn't need to worry about Bryce following us.

I didn't know where he was living, but I knew where he was working, and I was pretty sure he was still driving his beloved Range Rover.

I told Ethan about the PR firm and what their address was and then the make, model, and color of his car.

Ethan nodded curtly. "And do you know the license plate?"

I cringed a little. "HAILEY."

Ethan nearly choked on his eggs. "HAILEY?"

I nodded my head. "He made me get BRYCE as my plate. He's completely obsessed with me. I see that now."

Ethan didn't say anything, he just sighed and kissed the top of my forehead before going back to eating his breakfast.

THE CHRISTMAS HOLIDAY passed in a state of

pure bliss. No school, extra hours at work, and tons and tons of sexy time with Ethan.

By the time class was back in session, I was ready to rock and roll.

"Here's rent." I laid the crisp two hundred dollars on Ethan's workbench. He was hunched over a motorcycle. His leg was healing well; he was going to physical therapy like he should, and all that mess was behind us.

"Rent? You're my girlfriend now. That means we live together. I'm not collecting rent from you."

He looked shocked, shoving the money back at me.

I crossed my arms. "Ethan. No way. Take it. I'm pretty sure girlfriends pay their own way when couples live together."

He tucked the money in my pocket. "I'm sure they do when they buy a place together. I already had this place and I can afford it. Get some new nursing scrubs or something with it."

I pulled at my baggy blue scrubs. "What are you trying to say? You don't like the 'extra large on clearance' look?"

He grinned, using a wrench to tighten a bolt. "You look beautiful in anything. That's what I was trying to say."

"Good answer." I winked. "I'm working after class, so don't expect me until late."

He nodded. "Closing? I'll pick you up at 3AM."

I knew that picking me up at 3AM and then working at 8AM killed him. "You sure?"

He nodded.

"Alright, see you then. I'll text you if I'm off early." I bent down and kissed his cheek before pulling back to head for the door when he yanked me down to the floor with him and captured my mouth in a sexy kiss.

Laughter bubbled out of me. "I'm going to be late!" I lightly smacked his chest, wearing my perma-grin, the one I always had around Ethan.

He released me, but not before smacking my butt lightly and giving me a sexy wink. Coming home to this man every night was my own personal version of heaven.

"Oh, Hailey?" he called out after me.

I looked back at him. "What's up?"

"The boys and I put that tracker on Bryce's car. He sure spends a lot of time in this neighborhood driving around, so be safe."

My stomach dropped. They'd put it on already? I had forgotten to ask. He drove around this neigh-borhood?

This one?

I patted my bag, feeling the cold steel of the gun I'd stashed there, the one Ethan gave me for Christmas.

"I will." And with that I stepped outside, unable to shake the feeling that I was being watched. But something else brought me peace, because now Ethan was watching Bryce *and* I had a gun. If that bastard got within five feet of me I wouldn't hesitate to call the police and pull my weapon.

I was distracted all through class, thinking about Bryce and how he was interfering with my happily-ever-after. By the time my teacher dismissed us, I felt completely out of sorts.

"Wanna get together and start a study group for the NCLEX?" a studious friend Maureen asked as we walked out to the bike racks.

The NCLEX was the state nursing exam we needed to pass in order to become nurses, and although it was over a year away, you could never start studying for it too soon.

"Hell yes. Great idea," I told her. "Text me what days are good for you."

We hugged and said goodbye and then I started off on my bike. I had seven minutes to book it to the bus stop or I'd be late for work. I peddled hard through campus and cut down a side alley that would spit me out onto the main road that would lead to my stop. It was crazy how dead downtown got after 5PM. Peddling hard, I was so focused on getting to my bus stop that Bryce's voice startled me.

"Hailey." He popped out of the shadows and I swerved to keep from running right into him. Instead my bike slammed into the wall and I crashed. My body lurched forward, throwing me off the bike, and I landed hard on the cement. Pain exploded in my ankle and the entire left side of my body that had hit the wall.

My eyes flicked over to see Bryce walking towards me with something in his hand. Concern pulled at his features. "Shit, are you okay?"

He was sick. So very sick in the head. The entire left side of my leg was bleeding with road rash and my backpack was on my back. The one with my cellphone and gun in it. Now that Bryce was closer, I could see what he was holding.

A Taser.

I quickly slung my arm out of my backpack strap and tried to move the bag to the front so that I could get into the zipper, but realized I'd hurt my left arm. *Bad.* It might be broken. It was bleeding from road rash and hung there floppily as I cradled it to my chest.

Krav Maga was shit in this scenario. I was fucking hurt and my legs were tangled in my bike. I didn't know what to do.

"Bryce, please," I whimpered as panic flushed through me. "I just want you to leave me alone."

His concerned gaze vanished in an instant and was replaced with the grim expression of a killer.

He crouched down and wrapped his hand around my injured wrist, squeezing it. Pain like I'd never felt before flared to life, sharp and hot. It moved from my wrist up to my elbow as tears ran down my cheeks.

"Hailey..." He pulled the Taser close to my face and I whimpered. "Not to be cliché, but if I can't have you, then no one can." Before I could do anything, he shoved the Taser into my ribcage and my entire body convulsed. My head whipped back and cracked on the brick wall behind me and everything went black.

SIXTEEN

W hen I came to, that fight-or-flight instinct kicked in and my eyes flew open in panic. A headache the size of Texas throbbed at the base of my skull, but it was just a close second to the deep throbbing pain in my left wrist. I peered around frantically, trying to get my bearings. I was lying in the back seat of Bryce's car ... we were moving. It was then that I remembered that Ethan had the tracker on Bryce's car and it gave me one small shred of hope.

"Awake?" Bryce looked back at me from the front seat and I swallowed hard, trying to assess what the fuck was going on.

He's going to kill me.

My ribs hurt from where he Tased me, but I

didn't think they were broken. Looking down, I noticed that my ankles were tied together; so were my hands. He tied my forearms together with rope, avoiding my injured wrist.

How fucking thoughtful.

"Bryce. Where are we going?" I decided at this point that my ex-husband was a full-on narcissistic sociopath with major delusions of grandeur and I was going to have to just roll with it or he would hurt me worse.

He glanced back between the seats again and grinned at me. "Somewhere tropical. A surprise trip just like you used to love."

My stomach sank.

Bryce use to tell me to pack a bag and he'd take me on these wild and expensive vacations. All part of the plot to lure me in.

"Really?" My voice squeaked. "Right now? I haven't even packed my bag."

My bag. My backpack! Slowly sitting up—fuck, my ribs hurt—I peered in the cargo trunk area and sighed in relief at the sight of my bike and backpack.

Bryce looked at me through the rearview mirror. "I bought you all new things. Besides we won't be coming back to this shithole ever again. Best to leave that stuff behind."

Ever again.

"Bryce..." I hedged. "Why wouldn't we come back? I'm getting my nursing degree. It's really important to me—"

"You're so selfish!" he shouted suddenly, causing me to jump. "It's important to you. What about what's important to me. You never think about me."

He tipped the speedometer to ninety miles an hour and I was half tempted to reach my tied arms around his neck and fucking strangle him to death. But then I'd probably die in the roll-over. I wasn't buckled in.

"You're right. I'm sorry," I lied. I'd once found medication in Bryce's gym bag. I thought he'd been having an affair. He'd been acting so fucking evil to me I thought he must be going somewhere else for sex, but all I'd found was the bottle of pills. He'd nearly caught me, but I'd remembered the name. Later when Googling them, I'd learned they were antipsychotics, with an off-label use for depression. I figured he was depressed and chalked it up to that. Now I wondered ... Bryce had some major skeletons in his closet and he'd hidden them from me.

"You're right," I placated him. "I'm sorry. So how long will we be gone?"

He exited the I-10 and headed for a seedy part of

town, the ones where drug dealers and prostitutes lived.

His posture relaxed. "Forever. It's amazing what you can get for cash in Costa Rica. Right on the beach for less than fifty grand."

My heart knocked so loud in my chest I thought I might faint as adrenaline rushed through me.

Costa Rica.

"Wow. On the beach?" I tried to keep my voice even, not be too peppy because he would know that was fake. "But I don't have my passport."

He slowed the car to a crawl and pulled into a motel. There were a few prostitutes out front and my stomach rolled into knots. Bryce pulled around the back and parked the car. Only an old dude smoking a cigarette could be seen, and from the looks of him he wouldn't care what was going on here.

"I got us new passports, *Jane*." He reached into the glove box and handed me a passport.

With shaking fingers, I took the booklet in my tied-together hands and finagled it open.

My mouth popped open.

My picture, beside the name "Jane Green."

No, no, no.

I couldn't let him take me out of the country. I'd never be found again.

Bryce turned in his seat and looked at me. "I know we still have stuff to work through. But we will have all the time in the world once we get there. Just you and me and the beach."

His voice was so flat, so void of emotion … I think that's what scared me the most. "When does our plane leave? I cut myself in my bike fall. I'd like to clean up." I assumed he'd gotten a hotel room here, and if I could convince him to untie me and let me walk out of the car, I could make a run for it. At least make it to the front of the building, where the prostitutes might help me.

He frowned. "Yeah, sorry about this shithole. It's the only place that would take cash and didn't ask for ID. I'm still working on getting our social security numbers."

Oh my God, Oh my God.

"That's okay. Let's go inside and I'll shower real quick. I've got some make-up in my backpack," I lied. I had lip gloss in my backpack, but I needed that lie to get to my gun. I hoped he hadn't gone through it yet.

I held up my tied arms and he smiled. "You think I'm going to untie you out here?" He laughed and my stomach sank. "Babe, I got your email. I know how pissed you are at me. I know I can't trust you until you have shown me that you forgive me."

Tears flowed down my cheeks and I just nodded. I knew better then to argue with him at this point.

He stepped out of the car and went to the back, opening it for a second to grab my backpack and a large blanket. When he opened my door, I literally couldn't even kick him because my ankles were tied together. Instead I had to allow him to carry me, with the blanket covering my roped hands and feet. He had my backpack slung over his shoulder and another bag as well.

The old dude smoking looked over at us and Bryce smiled. "Newlyweds!" he shouted.

Then before I could decide whether or not I wanted to scream, he had the door open and waltzed inside, tossing me on the bed.

He locked the door quickly behind him and I craned my neck to try and see anything or anyone to help me.

When he saw me looking, a scowl marred his features. "You're not waiting for *Ethan*, are you?"

Ethan's name in his mouth was like poison.

He grinned and my stomach sank. "Because my private investigator told me about that tracker and I took it off my car before I picked you up. Drove around his neighborhood a bit first to taunt him."

I had been praying that he was watching the tracker and had seen Bryce get close to my school. That he would come save me, but now ... all hope was lost.

"Bryce," I whimpered, "please take these ropes off. I'm never going to be able to trust you again unless you treat me better."

His hand whipped out of nowhere and struck the side of my face, hard. "You trusting me? What about me trusting you? We go on a break and you go and fuck the first felon you can find?"

Anger flooded through my veins. Hailey 1.0 cowered when Bryce hit me, but Hailey 2.0 was enraged.

"A break? We are divorced, you sick fuck! Take these ropes off me and I'll show you how I really feel!"

My adrenaline was rushing through my body so fast that my legs shook. I shouldn't have said that; he was going to kill me. But instead of anger, intrigue crossed his face.

"Is that what you want? To hit me back? An eye for an eye and then we're good?"

Jesus Christ, I was getting whiplash from his

back and forth.

I nodded. "Would make me feel a hell of a lot better actually."

Pulling a knife from his pocket, he held it over my body and I flinched. There was something murderous in his eyes. Something that wanted me to attack him so he could kill me. It would give him reason to go all the way.

He sliced the ropes off my arms, looking at me like I was a specimen. Once my hands were free, I didn't move. I needed to play my cards right.

"Feet too please," I growled.

A small grin pulled at the corners of his mouth as he ran the knife down the binds on my ankles. One flick of my eyes and I calculated that my backpack was a mere five feet away. The top zipper was already open about five inches. I had to go for it. Otherwise I was either dead or on a flight to South America or God knows where, to live a life as Jane Green.

When he was cutting the last rope, his eyes flicked up to mine with a grin. The second the rope freed my foot. I yanked it back and Krav Maga'd his mother fucking face. My heel slammed into his cheek, sending him backward, and I launched off the bed, ignoring the pain in my body. In three seconds, I had my backpack in my hands and wrenched it open. Scrambling with my fingers inside, I searched for the black zipper gun case Ethan had gotten me.

"Looking for this?"

Click.

I closed my eyes for a moment and accepted my death right then and there.

I'd fucked up. I'd misjudged how smart he was, and now I was going to die.

Standing slowly, I turned to face him and stare down the barrel of my gun. Using the last weapon I had left.

"I still remember the first time we kissed," I muttered. "Homecoming, on the football field, raining. It was the best night of my life," I lied and took a tiny step closer. "My God, you were Bryce Conner and you picked me. I was so enthralled with you."

His face softened, and keeping the gun pointed at my chest, he nodded. "No one will ever love you as much as I do, Hailey. When will you see that?"

I nodded. "I see it now. I see that you're willing to kill me rather than let me go. That's the deepest love there is."

If I made it out of here, I was using my two hundred a month savings from living with Ethan rent free and going to therapy.

Another step closer.

Bryce smiled. "I remember taking your virginity. My parents were in Europe that summer."

I inwardly cringed at that memory. It had hurt and he'd been rough, not stopping when I whimpered, but I thought that was normal, that he'd been an eager hormonal teenage boy.

"Remember your proposal?" I laughed, really deserving a fucking Emmy award after this.

Three slow steps closer, the gun was lowering.

He defended himself: "I was so nervous, the words got jumbled!"

I was right near him and I decided to go for the kill. "We should have had a baby together. You would make an amazing father."

His eyes lit up, mouth going slack a little as he fully lowered the gun.

I took my chance then and leapt. I fucking jumped from where I stood knowing I had about five more feet to cover. My ankle was sprained too but I jumped, ignoring the pain. As I sailed through the air, he recoiled and tried to bring the gun up, but I was already on top of him. With a crash, I collided with him and we both went down. Tucking my left injured wrist in between our bodies, I tried to put out my right wrist and soften the landing. My head ended up smacking against his and we both groaned in pain.

I'd taken all of two Krav Maga classes.

Two.

I was on the floor with a man holding a gun that was trapped between our bodies and I had no idea what to do.

Krav Maga was all about powerful strikes, delivering deep blows to muscle or bone that shocked the system. My left wrist was out of the game, so I raised my right elbow and came down with every ounce of power I had, right on his collar bone.

He cried out in pain and I didn't let up. I pulled my body back and rammed my knee into his groin, causing him to curl into a ball.

Reaching down, I tried to yank the gun from his grip but he was strong.

"You bitch!" He spat in my face, and then out of nowhere he headbutted me so hard that blackness exploded behind my eyes and I was thrown off of him. Losing my grip on the weapon, I was completely thrown to the side.

Bryce started to stand up, shakily, like he was disoriented, and that's when I heard Ethan's voice.

"HAILEY! Are you here?!" Ethan's muffled, panicked voice sounded from outside the motel.

"ETHAN!" I shouted, feeling renewed strength.
I wasn't alone.

Scrambling to stand, dizziness washed over me but I fought through it, just as Bryce raised the gun.

"Your love turned me into a monster!" he declared just as the door burst open and the gun went off.

I flinched, grabbing my stomach as his blood splattered all over me.

Bryce had pulled the gun up to his chin in the last moment and blew his own head off. I grasped at my stomach, still in disbelief that he'd shot himself and not me.

My knees went weak as Ethan hurdled the bed and swam into view.

"Are you okay?" He looked back at Bryce's crumpled body and then stood before me, covering the bloody show from my view.

Sobs wracked my body, sirens blaring in the distance.

"Are you bleeding?" Ethan was running his hands all over me, checking my belly for wounds, then my neck, my arms.

I couldn't speak. I was in shock. Words weren't forming.

I just kept saying, "Oh my God, oh my God,"

over and over again as I sobbed.

"It's okay. I called the police when you didn't show to work. I had two trackers put on his car and he only found one."

Ethan pulled me from the room. We stood outside as half a dozen police cars pulled up, guns out.

Looking behind me, at Bryce's crumpled form, I thought that maybe he did really love me. At least in his own sick way. He loved me enough to kill himself and end my torture, and for that I was grateful.

I was strapped to a gurney; lights were flashed in my eyes. The word "shock" kept getting used; sirens, hospital, doctors, policemen. Through it all, one person never left my side, never let go of my hand.

Ethan.

Ethan was going to be there to help me pick up the pieces of my life. That was the only thing I was clinging to right now.

Ethan stroked my hair as I lay on his chest in the hospital room. "Shhh, you're safe now. You never have to worry about him again."

I was free of Bryce Conner. Free to live life on my terms without looking over my shoulder. With that final thought, I drifted off to sleep. My fingers intertwined with Ethan's.

EPILOGUE

I pulled a piece of lint off my graduation cap and handed the hat to Angela so she could pin it into my hair.

Her eyes were misty. "Girl, I'm so proud of you. First one of my friends to graduate college."

I smiled. "You've been a huge help to me this year. I seriously owe you everything."

The media had a field day with Bryce's kidnapping-turned-suicide-but-almost-murder. Rich boy kidnaps ex-wife charity case and takes her to seedy motel. It was all over the news for months. Angela would storm the news people who showed up to Mickey's or while we were out. She went on such foul-mouthed tirades that they couldn't put it on the air. Ethan was more methodical in his approach to dealing with the press. He bought a bunch of Super Soaker water guns and would soak the newswoman, her camera equipment, and anything else he could if they showed up at his shop.

I rubbed Angela's big pregnant belly. "I can't believe you're knocked up again," I laughed, because we'd been laughing about that oopsie for four months.

She held a bobby pin between her fingers. "Girl, I can't believe I'm knocked up again either. By the time you and Ethan are on your first kid, I'll be on my tenth."

A grin pulled at my lips. Cody had the shock of his life when she'd peed on the test and it was positive. But he'd come around and now they were excited for the baby. The thought of having babies with Ethan one day appealed to me. We were getting ready to celebrate our two-year anniversary together. We didn't of course count that little bit of time apart. His motorcycle shop was doing so well that he had decided to open a location in Tucson, near UofA, and hire a manager to run it. Things were going great.

I pulled out my phone and instinctively checked the app that managed his blood sugar.

98.

Stable.

"Nurse Hailey." Angela let the new title roll off her tongue and I couldn't stop smiling. I'd passed my NCLEX with flying colors and even had a job offer already. I would be working in an endocrinologist's office, helping kids with diabetes manage their disease. Going through the past two years with Ethan and dealing with the ups and down of diabetes inspired me to continue caring for others in that field. So much so that I had something else I wanted to talk to Ethan about tonight at my graduation party...

An announcement over the loudspeaker called all graduates to the auditorium and broke up my thoughts.

I popped up and pulled my only friend into a hug. "See you soon."

Her eyes were tearing. "So fucking proud of you!" she called after me, getting some glares from parents in the area.

I just grinned. That was Angela.

After slipping into the auditorium, I went to my seat. The rows were alphabetical and I'd practiced last night in the run-through. As I made my way to the chair with my name on it, I grinned at the single red rose I saw sitting there. Casting my gaze up to the crowd, I saw Ethan sitting with Sebastian, James, Angela, Cody, and Mickey.

He was grinning ear to ear and I gave him a big smile, trying not to cry.

They weren't my family by blood, but somehow I'd made my own family, just as Ethan said I would when I was younger. Family are those you choose to love unconditionally regardless of blood. I was so damn blessed to have this crew by my side.

The ceremony proceeded, and when they called my name, my little pack of wild family shouted with pride so loud it caused emotion to swell in my chest.

I'd done it. I'd put myself through school, paying every dollar of my tuition, books, and supplies with money I'd earned. All by myself.

After the ceremony, I followed the throng of students outside. There were hundreds of family members looking for their graduate, but mine was easy to spot. I just tracked the rip-roaring sound of the motorcycles and there they were. Standing at the edge of the curb in a black button-up shirt and black slacks with all-black converse shoes was my Ethan King. You'd think he was headed to a funeral in that outfit, but that was just his style. He'd never looked sexier. Shedding my cap and gown, I exposed my silk blue dress and black heels.

Ethan was watching me with this look of adoration. My new therapist liked Ethan, said he was stable and healthy for me. Not that I needed her approval, but it was nice to have.

"Nurse Hailey." He tipped his head to me, wearing a sexy grin.

I smiled, throwing my arms around him and let him spin me.

"I'm so incredibly proud of you," he breathed against my neck.

Tilting his head up, I took his face in my hands. "I couldn't have done this without you."

Leaning forward, I brushed my lips across his before Sebastian and Angela started their heckling.

James, as always, was silent.

"I have a graduation present for you," Ethan murmured, and I squealed. He set me down and I noticed that the boys had been standing in a wall formation, hiding something.

"Boys..." Ethan tipped his head to the side.

One by one, they moved out of the way and my mouth went slack. A powder-blue Vespa was leaning on its kickstand, right behind Ethan's bike.

I shrieked, "You said a Vespa would never be allowed in your garage!" I bounced up and down in excitement.

He shrugged. "I was thinking of making you park out back so you don't embarrass me."

I punched his arm lightly and he cracked a sexy grin.

"You got me a Vespa." Reaching out, I pulled him closer to me.

"You wanted one. I want you to have everything you want." His lips brushed mine and I thanked my lucky stars for this man. He was everything.

"Where's Mickey?" I looked around suddenly, realizing he wasn't there.

Ethan's eyes twinkled. "He had business at the bar. Sent his best wishes."

I knew they were throwing a surprise party for me there; Angela let it slip.

"Should we go there for a drink?" I asked innocently.

He nodded. "Great idea."

I'd promised Angela I would act shocked.

Climbing onto my new ride, I grinned at the silver glitter helmet Ethan had hung around the handle. He left first, with me right behind him and the boys behind me, all in a neat little line. I marveled at how far Ethan and I had come. His leg was fully healed; he was riding again, and I'd continued with the Krav Maga classes. My therapist thought it was a good idea. I now felt safe in any dark alley walking home from work. Not that Ethan would ever let me walk home.

The drive to Mickey's was short, and as we pulled up I recognized a few of the cars and motorcycles but pretended I didn't.

I bet they decorated with a sign, "Congrats Hailey" or something like that. I was so damn lucky to have these people in my life.

As I pulled the kickstand on my new ride, Ethan and I walked hand in hand to the door. Once he reached to open the door for me, I looked back at Angela and winked.

Time for me to act surprised.

The first thing I noticed was a banner strewn above the back of the bar.

The second thing was that no one had screamed surprise, and when my eyes flew to the banner, shock ripped through me as I read the words:

Marry Me Hailey.

White Christmas lights were zigzagged across the ceiling, setting a romantic vibe, and all of my friends and classmates were gathered around the bar, watching and filming my reaction.

I spun, looking at Ethan with my mouth popped open.

He was on one knee, and that's when the tears came.

"Hailey Willows, I simply cannot contemplate a life without you. Will you marry me and make me the happiest man on Earth?"

I could barely see him through my blurry tears. "Yes," I croaked out, only now aware that he was holding a ring box.

He whipped the ring out and slipped it on my finger. I barely had time to glance at the beautiful circle cut diamond before the bar erupted into cheers and Ethan pulled me into a hug.

I'd truly never felt so happy and hopeful for my future until now. Ethan's arms tight around me, this ring on my finger, it was all I ever wanted. Eternity with Ethan would not be enough.

Pulling back, he looked down at me. "What did I do to deserve you? I'm the luckiest man alive."

I smiled, remembering now that I needed to talk to him about something, especially if we were getting married. "Would you still feel lucky if I asked you to move to Tucson with me while I complete medical school?"

His mouth popped open and now it was my turn to surprise him.

"You got into medical school?" I was trying to

gauge his reaction, and by the grin on his face he was stoked.

I nodded. "Kind of. I didn't tell anyone because I'd be too embarrassed if I failed, but I've been accepted as a biology major at UofA. I can get my bachelors in two years with all of my nursing credits transferred. Then I'll pass my MCATS, and hopefully get accepted to UofA's medical school program. You could run the shop there while I specialize in pediatric endocrinology? I could work nights at the hospital as a nurse to try and pay some of the tuition, but I'm gonna have to figure the rest of the money part out because—"

He grabbed his chest. "I'm marrying a doctor! Holy shit, Scotty is gonna flip. Don't worry about the money. I'll get a loan against the shop if I have to."

"I'm not a doctor yet!" I laughed. "Is that a yes?" My stomach did flip flops.

"That's an absolute fucking yes. I'll follow you anywhere, Hailey."

Genuine happiness spread throughout my limbs. I was following my dreams, living up to my potential. The bad days were finally behind me.

It was only up from here.

I was free.

The End

STALK ME: But not like Bryce...

https://geni.us/fbleiastone

https://geni.us/bookbubleiastone

https://geni.us/twitterleiastone

https://geni.us/instagramleiastone

https://geni.us/amazonleiastone

IF YOU ENJOYED THIS STORY, you might also like these others by Leia Stone:

Matefinder

https://geni.us/matefinder

DEVI (MATEFINDER BOOK **2**)

https://geni.us/matefinder2

BALANCE (MATEFINDER BOOK **3**)

https://geni.us/matefinder3

KEEPER (MATEFINDER NEXT **Generation**

Book 1)

https://geni.us/matefinderng1

WALKER (MATEFINDER NEXT **Generation Book 2)**

https://geni.us/matefinderng2

LOGAN: **Dragons and Druids Prequel**

https://geni.us/loganprequel

SKYBORN (DRAGONS **and Druids Book 1)**

https://geni.us/skyborn1

EARTHBOUND (DRAGONS **and Druids Book 2)**

https://geni.us/earthbound2

MAGICTORN (DRAGONS **and Druids Book 3)**

https://geni.us/magictorn3

. . .

WATER BLESSED (WATER **Realm Series Book 1**)

https://geni.us/waterblessed1

DREAM WARS: **Rising 1**

https://geni.us/dreamwars1

DREAM WARS: **Domination 2**

https://geni.us/dreamwars2

PROTECTOR (NIGHT WAR **Saga Book 1**)

https://geni.us/nightwar1

DEFENDER (NIGHT WAR **Saga Book 2**)

https://geni.us/nightwar2

REDEEMER (NIGHT WAR **Saga Book 3**)

https://geni.us/nightwar3

. . .

Ash (Hive Trilogy Book 1)

https://geni.us/hive1

Anarchy (Hive Trilogy Book 2)

https://geni.us/hive2

Annihilate (Hive Trilogy Book 3)

https://geni.us/hive3

QUEEN HEIR (NYC MECCA **series Book 1)**

https://geni.us/nycmecca1

QUEEN ALPHA (NYC MECCA **Series Book 2)**

https://geni.us/nycmecca2

QUEEN FAE (NYC MECCA **Series Book 3)**

https://geni.us/nycmecca3

. . .

QUEEN MECCA (NYC MECCA **Series Book 4**)
https://geni.us/nycmecca4

MAGIC BITE (SUPERNATURAL **Bounty Hunter Series Book 1**)
https://geni.us/sbh1

MAGIC SIGHT (SUPERNATURAL **Bounty Hunters Series Book 2**)
https://geni.us/sbh2

FALLEN ACADEMY: **Year One**
https://geni.us/fallenacademyyearone

FALLEN ACADEMY: **Year Two**
https://geni.us/fayear2

FALLEN ACADEMY: **Year Three**
https://geni.us/fayear3

. . .

FALLEN ACADEMY: **Year Three And A Half**
https://geni.us/fayearthreeandhalf

FALLEN ACADEMY: Year Four
https://geni.us/fayear4

Made in the USA
Columbia, SC
26 April 2024

34943667R00183